## Praise for *The Christmas Blessing*

"Delightful prose and an affirming resolution will please readers."

*Publishers Weekly*

"Novelist Melody Carlson has written a deftly crafted, consistently entertaining, and ultimately inspiring story of love, hardship, and reconciliation that will leave readers filled with Christmas joy."

The Midwest Book Review

## Praise for *The Christmas Angel Project*

"Carlson's latest holiday offering is sure to become a fan favorite! Full of hope, it embodies all that is beloved about the Christmas season."

*RT Book Reviews*

## Praise for *The Christmas Joy Ride*

"No one captures the heartwarming fun of the Christmas season quite like Melody Carlson."

*USA Today*

"Popular and seasoned author Carlson skillfully draws readers into the lives of her characters; they, too, will feel like they are traveling along Route 66. Fans of Robin Jones Gunn and Catherine Palmer will surely find themselves snatching this quick Christmas read off the shelves."

*Library Journal*

"Uplifting and meaningful."

*RT Book Reviews*

# Books by Melody Carlson

*Christmas at Harrington's*
*The Christmas Shoppe*
*The Joy of Christmas*
*The Treasure of Christmas*
*The Christmas Pony*
*A Simple Christmas Wish*
*The Christmas Cat*
*The Christmas Joy Ride*
*The Christmas Angel Project*
*The Christmas Blessing*
*A Christmas by the Sea*

# *A* CHRISTMAS *by the* SEA

## MELODY CARLSON

Revell

*a division of Baker Publishing Group*
Grand Rapids, Michigan

© 2018 by Carlson Management, Inc.

Published by Revell
a division of Baker Publishing Group
PO Box 6287, Grand Rapids, MI 49516-6287
www.revellbooks.com

Printed in the United States of America

Library of Congress Cataloging-in-Publication Data
Names: Carlson, Melody, author.
Title: A Christmas by the sea / Melody Carlson.
Description: Grand Rapids, MI : Revell, a division of Baker Publishing Group,
    [2018]
Identifiers: LCCN 2017053948 | ISBN 9780800722715 (cloth : alk. paper)
Subjects: LCSH: Christmas stories. | GSAFD: Christian fiction.
Classification: LCC PS3553.A73257 C474 2018 | DDC 813/.54—dc23
LC record available at https://lccn.loc.gov/2017053948

18  19  20  21  22  23  24      7  6  5  4  3  2  1

# One

WENDY HARPER never considered herself a deceitful person. In fact, she was so scrupulously honest that it sometimes got her in trouble. Yet as she drove her jam-packed Subaru wagon over the Maine state line, she felt a gnawing sense of guilt. Maybe it was deceit by omission, but she knew it was wrong to let Jackson draw his own conclusions about their trip. Even if it was a convenient deception, she needed to convey the truth to her son. Without squelching his spirit—and hopefully before they reached their destination.

Wendy turned on the wipers, praying there wasn't snow in the drops pelting her windshield. It was late November, and although Ohio had been unseasonably warm when they'd left home, she knew that weather could change in an instant on the eastern seaboard. She glanced over to see that Jackson had drifted off. He might be a preadolescent, but he always appeared younger and more vulnerable while sleeping. Of course, his sweet innocence only added to her mother lode of guilt. She resisted the urge to adjust his oversized glasses, currently resting cockeyed on his straight freckled nose, or to remove his bright blue earbuds. Best to let sleeping boys lie.

Wendy knew her twelve-year-old was on the cusp of manhood. He was already as tall as her, and his voice had recently grown a bit deeper and cracked occasionally. Her best friend, Claire, claimed it was because Jackson was trying too hard to grow up and take his father's place. "He confided something to me last summer when he was helping me with yard work," Claire had disclosed just days ago. "He said Edward told him he'd have to become the *man of the house* . . . you know, after . . ."

Wendy had been both surprised and dismayed to hear this. It was hard to believe her husband would say such a thing to a child. What a heavy load to lay on a nine-year-old. Yet it did explain Jackson's change of interests these past couple of years—giving up soccer and lacrosse, spending more time at home. She loved that he was reading more but hated seeing him turn into a young hermit.

Jackson had even begged Wendy for home school, claiming he could keep up with his studies online. Worried about social isolation and lack of supervision, Wendy had promised to make this decision *after* Christmas. He'd protested, but a phone call from her grandfather's attorney provided the perfect distraction. Although Poppa had passed away last summer, Wendy had never expected him to leave her his beach cottage in Maine. When Jackson heard the news, he acted like they'd won the lottery! Even though she was touched by Poppa's generosity, her only goal was to get the property sold ASAP.

"We gotta go there!" Jackson had declared. At first she balked, knowing they couldn't afford the round-trip airfare or the time a drive from Ohio to Maine and back would require. But Jackson kept pushing until she finally gave in. Taking a few days off work during Thanksgiving week sounded doable—and that way she could personally meet the Realtor, list the house, and hopefully sell the cottage quickly. That money would help her and Jackson immensely.

The decision to drive to Maine was like a tonic for Jackson. A whole new boy, he'd even quit complaining about school. Of course, she eventually discovered that was because he'd been telling everyone that they were permanently relocating to Seaside, Maine. Despite her telling him to pack only enough for two weeks, he'd shoved everything he could fit into every crevice of her old Subaru. But his erroneous assumption had been so transformative that she'd simply kept her mouth shut. She just couldn't bear to rain on his happy parade. Oh, she attempted to dissuade him a few times. She'd warned him that the beach cottage was just a summer place that would be freezing cold in winter. But Jackson, ever the online researcher, insisted they could weatherize it themselves.

"And I can chop firewood and fix things," he'd offered. Every obstacle she tossed his way was soundly batted back with stubborn youthful optimism. Even when she described the house as a tiny, run-down shack—probably dilapidated, rodent infested, and rotting—he totally dismissed her concerns. And as she'd stuffed the last box into the back of the Subaru, she'd noticed Edward's old toolbox wedged in a corner.

Wendy glanced at her rearview mirror to see the stacked boxes and bags filling the back of her car. Unsure of what they'd find in the neglected cabin, she'd packed everything but

7

the kitchen sink. And since her boss had generously granted her additional vacation time, they would be in Seaside for a while. Almost until Christmas.

Of course, her packing and preparations had simply bolstered Jackson's confidence that they were "gone for good." And with each passing mile, his excitement and optimism had grown. While it made him a congenial traveling companion, it made her increasingly uneasy. She really needed to get him to understand their real purpose.

In his enthusiasm, Jackson had gone online, researching all he could find about Seaside and the Maine coast. Now he was convinced that he would learn to fish and sail . . . and to surf next summer. The more he'd shared his hopeful dreams the harder it became to disclose the whole truth. She hinted when she got the chance, but how could she admit that the real purpose of this trip was to spend a few weeks fixing up the beach cottage—then *sell* it? It would crush him.

Wendy didn't know the real value of Poppa's beach cottage, but even if it was a dilapidated wreck, which was possible, she felt certain the beachside location would be enough to wipe out the medical bills that insurance didn't cover and provide a small safety net for her and Jackson. If she was lucky it might even pay off their student loans and seed a small college fund for Jackson. She was probably overly optimistic, but no matter what, it would help.

She never discussed finances with Jackson, but Edward's battle with cancer had left her deep in debt. Even after selling their home, which had little equity, and moving to an "affordable" apartment, she'd been unable to climb out. Edward hadn't worked long enough before getting sick to have much in social security benefits. Certainly not enough to support them. So inheriting Poppa's sea cottage felt like a gift from God—just what they needed to get back on their feet. She was determined, no matter how much Jackson loved it and protested, the cottage must be sold.

Jackson suddenly sat up, giving her a start. "Are we there yet?" He chuckled at his own gaffe. "Sorry, Mom—you warned me not to say that again."

"Well, as it turns out, we passed the Maine state line around noon and—"

Jackson let out a happy whoop. "You should've woken me up. How much longer till Seaside?"

"I really hope to get there before dark. Why don't you check the GPS and tell me our ETA." She knew how Jackson liked acronyms.

Within seconds, he reported that they would arrive at their destination in three hours and seven minutes. "According to my calculations, that will be about 3:54," he declared. "Unless we stop."

"Well, I do need a pit stop and we need gas. I don't think Seaside even has a gas station," she told him.

"And I'm kinda hungry."

"We'll grab a quick bite and eat it in the car to save time."

"Sunset is supposed to be at 4:09," he told her. "That's because Maine is so far north. The shortened daylight time might take some getting used to, but I heard the long summer days make up for it. Do you know that the astronomical twilight lasts until almost eleven o'clock in late June? That'll be so cool."

"I don't know what an astronomical twilight is, but I do remember very late summer evenings." She grimaced to think of how he'd never get to experience that.

"Did you go to Seaside *every* summer as a kid?" he asked with interest.

"Every summer I can remember. Well, until I was seventeen. I had a job that summer—and then it was college and the distractions that came with it."

"Like getting married?" he teased.

"Right. After graduation, Dad and I moved to Cincinnati for his work. And not long after that, you came along, and, well, life just got busier and busier." She remembered how she used to long for Seaside, like clockwork, every summer—even more so when it got hot and humid in Ohio.

"So you haven't been back in almost twenty years? That's like a whole 'nother lifetime, Mom."

"Seems like it to me too. But even so, I can remember every bit of it like yesterday."

"Tell me more about it, Mom. You haven't really given me that many details."

She considered how to paint this picture without making it too rosy—or being disingenuous. "Well, the ocean is beautiful. That obviously won't have changed. And you'll see it soon enough."

"What about our house, Mom? And don't tell me it's falling down."

"The house . . ." She imagined the picturesque cottage with its weathered cedar shingles and white painted trim. "Well, I do recall the toilet had to be flushed twice . . . and the musty smell of the back porch and how the front porch sagged a little."

"Tell me something *good*, Mom."

"Let's see . . . the living room had this massive rock fireplace. I think my great-grandfather built it. The stonework was really pretty . . . although the fire would smoke up the house on a windy day." She sighed. "But the truth is I loved that smell. It would seep into my clothes, kind of like being around a campfire. And then there was my little dormer bedroom. It was tiny, but I loved it. My window looked out over the sea." She smiled at Jackson. "In fact, you can use that room if you like." Although she wasn't eager to take occupancy of her grandparents' downstairs bedroom, it would be the "grown-up" thing to do.

"Awesome!" He nodded. "Tell me more about our house."

"My next-favorite room was probably the kitchen. It had a big old gas stove and a linoleum floor that squeaked when you walked. There were buttery yellow cabinets and blue-and-white checked curtains on the windows. And Gammi used to make the best clam chowder—from clams that we dug ourselves. I hope I can find her recipe."

"How old were you when your grandma died?"

"I was in college," she said sadly.

"And then your parents died right after that?" His voice was laced with longing and she felt bad for the way her son had been deprived of extended family. Edward's parents had their own busy lives down in Fort Lauderdale, and hers had been killed in the car wreck.

"It was a few years later—you weren't even one when my parents died."

"But you must've been close to your grandpa? I mean, since he left you his beach house."

"I never thought that we were close, exactly. Poppa was a pretty stern man. At least I thought so when I was little. He always seemed very serious and set in his ways. But he did love to go fishing—and sometimes he took me with him."

She hadn't even told Jackson about Poppa's boat, but she doubted it was still around. "I do know that Poppa loved me. And he really loved Gammi. I never doubted that. But I spent most of my time with Gammi. She was always willing to go down to the beach with me, or ride bikes into town. And on a rainy day, she could always come up with something fun to do—card games, puzzles, baking. She was a very good artist and taught me a lot about painting."

"Maybe that's why you're such a good artist, Mom."

"Well, that's an overstatement . . . but maybe someday I'll have time to take it up again."

"So it was just you and your grandparents there—for the *whole* summer every summer?"

"Sometimes Aunt Kay and Uncle Rob and my cousin, Larry, would come. But they never stayed long." She chuckled. "But that was fine with me since Larry and I never really got along too well."

"Why not?"

"I don't know . . . I guess he wasn't interested in outdoor things."

"Not interested?" Jackson frowned.

"He never wanted to *do* anything. He didn't want to go fishing or clamming or shell gathering. I couldn't even get him to build a sandcastle with me."

"Sounds pretty boring."

"Yeah. I always felt relieved when they went home."

"What about your parents? Did they ever go to Seaside with you?" He sounded intent on fitting all the puzzle pieces of this fragmented family together.

"Not much. They both had their work and their lives in the city. My mom would show up sometimes on a weekend, you know, since Gammi and Poppa were her parents. But I always got the impression she was just putting in her time. She didn't like being there. She'd complain about the wind or the dampness or how sand was in everything. Plus my mom didn't like seafood at all. And Poppa loved fishing almost better than anything. That's about all we ate. Probably one reason I love all kinds of seafood now."

"Well, your grandpa must've loved you a lot, Mom, to leave his cottage to you like he did."

"I think he knew how much I enjoyed being there. He left his other house, in upstate New York, to my cousin, Larry. And since there were only two grandkids, I suppose it seemed fair to leave the cottage to me." She felt a different wave of guilt now, wishing she'd taken Jackson to Seaside sooner . . . while his great-grandfather was still living. Although she'd faithfully sent cards and letters and photos to Poppa, she'd never been able to make the trip back there. Certainly she'd had plenty of good excuses—work and life demands and then Edward's illness. But now it was too late.

"What was your most favorite thing about summers in Seaside?"

"My most favorite thing?" She considered this. "With so many wonderful memories, it's hard to say. I loved just being at the cottage with Gammi. I also enjoyed getting ice cream in town . . . and fishing with Poppa . . . but my most favorite thing was probably the beach itself. Seaside has a good shell-collecting beach. I loved going out early in the morning, searching for treasures."

"Yeah, I read about the beach. It sounds cool."

"And my grandparents were fabulous beachcombers. The

cottage was full of all sorts of shells and sea glass and whatever they'd drag home after a storm."

"Do you think they're still there? The shells and stuff?"

"Oh, I don't know . . . I hope so." Seeing the rain had stopped, she turned off the wipers. "I'd always hoped to find a sand dollar on that beach." She noticed signage for the town up ahead and turned on her signal to exit. "But I never found a single one. Gammi and Poppa only had three sand dollars. They kept them up on the mantel. Hopefully, they're still there."

As Wendy pulled into the gas station and convenience market, she felt a small rush of excitement. Maybe this was what Jackson felt—the eager anticipation for what lay ahead. As they emerged from the car, she got a whiff of what smelled like pungent sea air—or maybe it was her imagination. But in the same instant, she felt the child inside her waking up, demanding to know: *Are we there yet?* Was it really possible that her beloved Seaside was only a few hours away?

Fortified with chicken tenders, potato skins, and drinks, Wendy and Jackson hurried back to the car just as the sky opened up and let loose another deluge of cold, pounding rain. As Wendy started the engine, turning the wipers on full blast, her earlier enthusiasm waned considerably. Her plan to disclose the truth to Jackson *before* their arrival loomed above her—just like the dark clouds overhead.

"This is the best day ever," Jackson declared as he dipped a piece of chicken in the barbecue sauce. "I haven't felt this good since . . . well, you know."

She *did* know. So maybe it was okay to live in a delusion—even if only for a short while. Didn't she and Jackson deserve a small measure of happiness? Even if it was only temporary

. . . or delusional? Jackson deserved a break from his middle-school tormenters—and no one could deny that Wendy was overdue for a vacation. Even her boss acted eager for her to go. "Just be back by December 23rd," he'd reminded her on Friday. "I've planned an important full-day staff conference—a meeting of the minds and a bit of a holiday party. I want you there too."

That gave them a little more than three weeks—plenty of time to fix up the cottage and place it on the market. Hopefully it wouldn't even take that long. The bigger question was, how long would it take for Jackson to realize how small and isolated Seaside truly was . . . and how dead and boring it could get when winter set in? A generous dose of disillusionment might be just the ticket to get him to change his mind about becoming a permanent resident there. She could only pray.

# Two

DESPITE HER RESOLVE not to surrender to childish feelings of delight over her belated return to Seaside, Wendy let out a happy gasp as they reached the outskirts of the small coastal town. The heaviest clouds had continued westward and the sinking sun was now painting the sky in vibrant shades of coral, purple, and amber.

"Oh, my!" She pulled the car onto the road's shoulder. "I've got to get a photo of this gorgeous sunset." She grabbed up her phone and hopped outside, snapping a couple of good shots.

"Seaside is welcoming us," Jackson exclaimed.

"Maybe so." She zoomed her phone's camera toward the eastern horizon.

"Is that the ocean?" Jackson pointed to the barely visible dark blue strip of water.

"Yes," she said. "That's it."

He let out another happy whoop then swooped her into a big bear hug. "This is so cool, Mom! I think I can smell the ocean."

She sniffed the air then nodded. "I can smell it too. There's nothing like the scent of the sea." She felt herself choking back unexpected tears. Were they tears of joy or sadness? She wasn't sure, but to distract herself she took a few more photos, then got back in the car.

"Maybe you can paint something from those pictures," Jackson suggested as she continued driving toward town.

"I probably couldn't do it justice," she confessed. "Skies are hard to replicate."

"WELCOME TO SEASIDE," Jackson triumphantly read from the sign. "POPULATION 2058." He laughed. "About to become 2060!"

She grimaced.

"Seaside is more than a hundred times smaller than Cincinnati—and that's just fine with me." He pointed to a big gleaming SHELL sign. "Hey, you're wrong, Mom, they *do* have a gas station."

"Well, Seaside is definitely bigger than it was." She peered at what used to be the outskirts of town, now filled in and built up. "But I'd still call it a one-horse town."

"One horse is enough for me." He leaned forward, looking left and right as she slowly cruised down Main Street. Despite being off-season, the town still looked surprisingly sweet and welcoming—and not completely vacated.

"Looks like they've done some improvements," she quietly conceded.

"Oh, Mom, it's way better than I expected!" He pointed out some highlights—the ice cream shop, the old arcade, the chowder house, a bowling alley that was new to her, and finally the wharf where dozens of boats were bobbing in the water. "This is so cool, Mom. What more could we want in a town?"

"Well, there's no denying this place has grown and changed some," she admitted.

"Maybe it's a *two*-horse town now."

"Maybe." She stopped at the intersection where Main Street and Beach Avenue crossed, looking around. "But, as you can see, not everything is open. That's how it is in the off-season." She pointed at the darkened Fisherman's Wharf restaurant as evidence.

"But it's a Monday, Mom. Lots of places aren't open on Mondays—even in the city."

"Yes, I suppose that's true."

"That's open." He pointed to a grocery store on Beach Avenue, also new to her. "You said to remind you to get some groceries."

She turned into the parking lot. "Yes, we need eggs and milk and a few perishable things. Let's be quick though. I'd like to make it to the cottage and get everything unloaded before dark."

"Listen!" Jackson exclaimed as they walked across the parking lot.

"What?" She looked all around.

"I can hear it!"

"What?" She frowned.

"The ocean!"

She stopped walking long enough to listen, and sure enough the low rumble of the surf could be heard. "You're right," she whispered. "That's the ocean. Sounds a little rough out there too. Guess that's the edge of the storm we just drove through."

"Wow—that is so cool." He happy-danced up to the store.

They went inside, hurrying through a surprisingly well-stocked modern grocery store. Nothing like the stores she remembered from her last time here—and that had been in summer. They quickly gathered what they needed for tonight and tomorrow, but as they headed for the checkout, Wendy couldn't help but notice the colorful displays set up for Thanksgiving, showing off dressing mixes, canned pumpkin, cranberry sauce—as if the town hadn't evacuated for the off-season. She wondered what she and Jackson would be doing by Thursday—if the cabin was uninhabitable, they might even be on their way back home.

"New to town?" the young cashier asked pleasantly.

"Sort of." Wendy ran her plastic card through the machine, trying not to obsess over how she'd covered all the expenses of this trip with credit so far. But once the cottage was sold, she would easily pay it all off.

"Mom used to come here as a girl," Jackson proudly told the cashier.

"My grandparents had a beach cottage, just down the road a ways." She signed her name.

"But they died," Jackson declared. "And now it's *our* beach house and we're going to live there."

"Well then, welcome to Seaside—I'll look forward to seeing you guys in here again." The young woman smiled brightly.

"Yeah." Jackson grinned as he picked up the bag. "We'll probably be back to get more groceries—a lot. But we gotta hurry to our house before dark."

Wendy smiled stiffly and thanked the cashier. Somehow she needed to get Jackson to understand their situation better. Maybe later tonight, after they got settled in.

"Does everything look familiar?" Jackson asked as she turned the car back onto Beach Avenue.

"Parts of it are. But that grocery store is new." Then she pointed to a large three-story structure. "*That* is definitely new."

"Seaside Hotel," Jackson read from the sign. "Looks like a nice place."

"I guess." Hopefully they wouldn't have to return to spend the night here. She knew the beach cottage might be uninhabitable—and perhaps it would be a blessing in disguise since that would force her to just sell the land and head back to Ohio. Relieved to see a Vacancy sign, she continued down the beach road. There were more houses than the last time she'd been here. Much bigger than the old cottages, probably more expensive too. But maybe that was good—perhaps real estate was on the rise.

"Are you excited, Mom?"

"Excited?"

"You know, about being back here? It must be pretty cool after such a long time."

"Yeah . . ." She sighed. "Pretty cool." She remembered the feeling when Poppa would drive them down this same road for the first time in summer. It was usually mid-June, shortly after school ended. "When we used to come here, back when I was a girl, we'd usually get here late in the day. We'd all unload the car, and eventually we'd have a late dinner out on the deck, overlooking the ocean. Poppa loved to watch the sunset. Our first day here always felt magical to me."

"It feels magical to me too," Jackson said quietly.

"Gammi had a neighbor friend, Mrs. Campbell, who always knew when to expect us. She'd go over and open up the house for us that morning. She'd air it all out and put out fresh linens—even stock a few things in the fridge. And sometimes, if it was cool, she'd build us a welcoming fire in the fireplace."

"Pretty nice neighbor. You think she's still around?"

"Oh, I doubt it. Seemed like she was pretty old back then. She'd probably be about a hundred by now."

"Are we *almost* there?"

Wendy poked him in the shoulder.

"Sorry, Mom. It's just that I'm so excited to see the cottage. It feels kinda like Christmas, you know?"

"I do know." She also knew they'd be home by Christmas. Hopefully Jackson would be over it by then.

"Don't tell me when you see it, Mom. I want to guess. Okay?"

"Sure." She'd already shown him an old photo of the shingle-covered two-story house, with herself as a scrawny preadolescent, standing in her swimsuit on the sagging front porch. But it wasn't much different than a lot of these summer cottages. When she spotted the house, she was pleasantly surprised—it didn't look quite as ramshackle as she'd imagined. Even the porch looked straighter and sturdier than she remembered.

"That's it," Jackson declared, pointing at the grayed structure with white trim.

"You got it right." She turned into the driveway.

"What's that white stuff on the driveway?" he asked.

"Crushed oyster shells," she explained. "It's Maine gravel."

"Cool."

"Looks like someone fixed the front porch," she observed as she parked.

"Look, Mom, there's a light inside. And smoke from the chimney. Think it's a ghost?"

"I, uh, I don't know." Wendy stared at the structure. Was this the wrong house?

"Maybe your grandma's neighbor is still around."

"Oh, I don't think so." She felt uneasy as she turned off the engine. What if someone had snuck in and was squatting? She'd heard of vacation cabin break-ins. Was it unsafe to take her son inside? "Hold on," she told Jackson as he opened the door.

"Why?" He already had one foot out. "This is *our* house, isn't it?"

"Yes, but . . . I don't understand what's going on." She reached for her phone. "I spoke to Poppa's attorney last week, telling him we were coming. He told me where the key was hidden, but I wonder if someone found—"

"Who's that?" Jackson pointed to an elderly woman who had come out of her house and was shuffling toward them in her bedroom slippers and waving with enthusiasm.

"Mrs. Campbell!" Wendy got out of the car and hurried over to greet the old woman. "I can't believe you're still here."

"Wendy!" Mrs. Campbell opened her arms, hugging her warmly. "I'm so happy to see you." She turned to Jackson. "This must be your son, Jackson. Your grandpa showed me pictures of him, but land sakes, he's bigger than you." She patted Jackson on the shoulder. "Almost a full-grown man."

"I'll be thirteen in April," he told her.

"Must be tall for your age."

"Takes after his dad," Wendy said.

"Can I go see the beach now?" Jackson begged. "Before it's too dark?"

"Yes, of course." Wendy looked out over the dusky dune

that dropped down to the surf. "Just don't wander far. I don't want you getting lost on your first day here."

"And there's no moon tonight," Mrs. Campbell warned. "It'll be pitch-black soon." She pointed out the lamppost by the beach trail, explaining that he could see it from the beach, and then Jackson took off running.

"Did you make a fire for us?" Wendy asked.

"Truth be told, I had help." Mrs. Campbell linked arms with Wendy, walking up to the front porch with her. "My brother Harvey lives with me. He made the fire."

"Thank you both! But how did you know we were coming today?"

"Your grandpa's lawyer phoned me last week." She glumly shook her head. "I was so sad to hear about his passing last summer. So sorry for your loss, dear."

"Thank you."

"Anyhow, the lawyer knew all about me and how your grandpa paid me to look after the house in the off-season. I told him I'd hide my key for you." She pointed to a flowerpot by the door. "It's right there."

Wendy extracted the key, slipping it into the lock.

"Anyhow, we expected you here on Saturday, so Harvey made a fire that morning and I got a few things ready for you, but then you didn't show. So he made another fire yesterday—and then today."

"I told the attorney we were leaving on Saturday so he probably assumed we were flying, but I drove. Anyway, it was so kind of you to do that!" Wendy peered at the old woman's face in the porch light, trying to determine her age. Certainly, not a hundred, but she had to be in her late eighties.

"Good thing too. Place was cold as ice on Saturday. Took

two days just to get the chill off, but it oughta stay nice for you. Especially since your grandpa got it insulated a few years ago. I just turned the heaters off—didn't want to waste electricity since the place was already warm—but you might want to put them back on before you go to bed. And I got Harvey to turn on the water for you too." She waited for Wendy to open the front door. "Sorry I didn't get fresh linens on the beds. My arthritis has troubled me something fierce these past few winters. But I did stock you some provisions in the fridge. Not much, mind you, but some of my homemade huckleberry jam and a few other goodies."

"That sounds wonderful." Wendy hugged her again. "You're the best, Mrs. Campbell."

"I s'pect it was a long trip for you." She nodded with satisfaction. "I just wanted you to feel welcome."

"That was so kind." Wendy glanced around the living room to see the same worn plaid sofa, Gammi's antique oak rocker, Poppa's old leather recliner, and numerous other pieces. But the walls looked different. Instead of the old panels of dark wood with exposed studs, they were covered in unpainted beaded board. "Looks like some improvements have been made."

"Your grandpa'd been fixing the place up some these past few years." Mrs. Campbell sadly shook her head. "I s'pect he knew he wasn't long for this world and wanted to make it nicer for you and your boy." She led Wendy through the house, pointing out various improvements.

"Looks like he thinned a few things out too," Wendy observed. "Not quite as much clutter as I remember." She picked up a conch shell. "But I'm relieved to see that the shells are still here."

"Your grandpa turned that upstairs spare bedroom into a storage room," Mrs. Campbell told her. "I'm afraid it will be a bear to clean out."

"That's okay. I expected to find a ton of work here. I'm pleasantly surprised it's not far worse."

"Well, don't fool yourself. There's still plenty to do. Harvey claims your bathroom floor is spongy. Hope your toilet don't fall through." She shook a warning finger at her. "You just walk softly and call yourself a handyman in the morning. I left a business card from the fellow who used to do work for me before Harvey came to help. I highly recommend Gordon. He's a good man and being it's wintertime he shouldn't be too busy."

They visited a bit longer. Then, seeing the sky was getting dark, Wendy escorted her elderly neighbor down the porch steps and across the driveway. "Thank you again for all your help." She glanced at her slippers. "Do you need me to walk you back to—"

"Land sakes, no. I'm just fine on my own."

Wendy told her good night. Then, relieved to see her son sprinting up the beach trail, she started to extract a box from the back of the car.

"Let me unload the car, Mom," Jackson said breathlessly.

She stepped back, using the car's light to take in his wind-blown hair, flushed cheeks, and happy smile. Besides looking almost grown, he wasn't the same boy from back in Ohio. "But I can carry some—"

"I can do it, Mom." He flexed a bicep then reached across her to get the box, setting it down on the driveway. "Just let me."

"So how was the beach?" She watched as he loosened

up some of the other things, acting like he had this under control.

"Awesome! I can't wait to see it in the daylight. I need to check the tide table."

"This one's mine." She reached for her overnight bag, tugging it out. "I'll take it inside."

"Okay, but only that one," he warned. "I'll get the rest of this."

"But there's so much—"

"Just go inside, Mom. Give yourself a break."

"But I—"

"I *want* to, Mom." He gave her a firm nudge. "I'll bring stuff into the house and you can put it wherever it goes from there."

"Thanks, Jackson." There was no denying her son was growing up. Whether it was from his determination to be "the man of the house" like Claire had said, or just something natural and inevitable, it was happening fast—and she doubted there was much she could do to prevent it. But it was bittersweet. Although part of her felt pleased and proud, another bigger part felt like sobbing.

# Three

THIS PLACE is way cool!" Jackson exclaimed as he carried the last loaded laundry basket inside. "I don't know why you dissed on it so much, Mom. It looks great to me. And that fireplace is epic—it's nice and warm in here. You said it'd be freezing cold."

"Well, it seems Poppa made some improvements since I was last here." Wendy knocked on a wall. "He even put in insulation."

"Awesome." Jackson followed her to the kitchen, pausing by the windowsill to admire the shells lining it. "These seashells are so cool, Mom. They're all over the house. Did your grandparents really find all of them right here on this beach? Do you think we can find some too?"

"Yes, of course. But remember my grandparents found these over the course of many decades. And for all I know it started out even before them. This cottage was here even before Poppa was born."

"When was it built?"

She considered this. "Well, Poppa was close to ninety

when he died . . . so I suppose the cottage could've been built around a hundred years ago."

"Where's my room?"

"Upstairs—the one on the right—with a bed."

"There are *two* bedrooms upstairs?"

"Yes, but the other one's being used for storage." She sighed to think how long it might take her to sort through all the junk she'd spied stacked in there. "Your room is better. Remember, it's the one that looks out over the sea."

"Cool." He grabbed up his duffle bag and backpack and clomped up the steep wooden stairs, whistling as he went.

"I'll have some dinner ready in about twenty minutes," she called after him. As she washed her hands, she gazed blankly out the kitchen window. Although it was black as ink out there, she could imagine the ocean not too far off. But with all traces of dusky light gone, she could only see her own reflection in the glass. She peered curiously at her image—surprised at how old and haggard she looked. So different from the girl she'd been during her last visit here. She pushed a strand of dark hair away from her forehead, staring with fascination at the older woman looking back at her. There were shadows beneath her dark brown eyes, and she knew the past two nights spent in uncomfortable motel beds hadn't helped. Her long hair pulled tightly back into a ponytail might be low-maintenance, but it wasn't very flattering. Plus, she'd taken a vacation from the "natural" makeup she usually wore. All added up to a forlorn-looking "elderly" woman who was actually only thirty-six. She pulled the faded gingham café curtains closed and turned away.

Releasing a weary sigh, she put away the groceries and started making a simple dinner. She might be tired, but at least they'd made it. Her biggest fear had been a breakdown in the Subaru or that one or more of her old tires would give out. But here they were—and the cottage was in better shape than she'd hoped for. With just a few improvements, some thinning, and fresh paint, she ought to be able to get a good price for it.

Wendy layered slices of bread with ham and cheese, then set an old cast-iron frying pan on the propane stove. Cautiously striking a match—and praying the big propane tank out back wasn't empty—she turned the knob just like Gammi had taught her. To her relief, it soon fired up and the pan began to heat. She buttered the outside of the bread, then laid in three sandwiches—two for Jackson and one for her. While they sizzled, she sliced up some carrots and apples and put the teakettle on for tea.

This was nothing like the delectable dinners Gammi used to pack for their first night at the beach, but then they weren't going to be eating out on the porch in the summer sunset either. Those days were gone, and everything was different now. Except for one pleasantly familiar thing. Despite her general tiredness and usual anxiety, Wendy felt that old sense of peace, a sensation she'd experienced each summer when spending time with her grandparents—that she was home . . . and safe.

Later in life, she'd felt like that with Edward. But it had evaporated when he'd been diagnosed with pancreatic cancer four years ago. She'd tried to re-create the feeling with Jackson. She'd imagined they would find that place again. But it always seemed just out of reach. So this unexpected emotion caught her off guard. So much so that she grew slightly uncomfortable—she wasn't quite sure how to handle the pleasant feeling.

"That bedroom is fantastic," Jackson announced as he bounced into the kitchen. "Are you sure you don't want it, Mom?"

"No, I'd rather be down here." Okay, this was partly a lie—she'd always loved her second-floor bedroom with its sloped ceiling and dormer window. But her protective-mother instincts felt Jackson was safer up there. Besides, she loved that he appreciated it.

"Then, if you don't mind, I'll box up your stuff and bring it down."

"Okay." She tried to remember what she might've left here as a sixteen-year-old—hopefully nothing too embarrassing.

"That smells good." Jackson pulled out a metal kitchen chair and sat down at the table. "I'm starved."

"I made you two sandwiches." She set his plate in front of him, followed by a tall glass of milk.

"Looks good." He waited for her to join him, then they both bowed their heads and she prayed a quick blessing like she usually did before their evening meals.

"And bless this house," Jackson said heartily. "And our new lives here too. Amen." He grinned, then took a big bite of his sandwich.

Wendy forced a smile, focusing her attention on dipping her tea bag in hot water. She admired his enthusiasm but at the same time felt deceptive. Maybe this was her big moment, her chance to tell him the truth—to confess the real reason they were here.

"I checked the weather app on my phone," he said between bites. "It's supposed to be pretty nice for the next few days. Maybe we can go beachcombing tomorrow."

She nodded as she chewed, reminding herself that this

visit was twofold—part work and part vacation. Perhaps it was best to focus on the vacation bit first. After all, the cottage was in much better shape than she'd hoped. "I'd love to spend some time on the beach," she told him. "But remind me to call a handyman first." She explained about the floor in the bathroom. "So don't go tromping around in there. You don't want to fall through."

"Maybe we can fix it ourselves," Jackson said with confidence. "That'd probably save a bunch of money."

"Oh, I doubt we can attack something that big all by ourselves."

"But I've got Dad's tools, and I can look for how-to help online."

"I don't think so, Jackson. That's the only bathroom in the house. The best plan is to get someone in here—and get it fixed fast." She looked around the kitchen, which was in need of a good scrub, new paint, and probably some new linoleum to make it more sellable. "But don't worry, there will be plenty of other work for us to do in here. And don't forget, we haven't really seen the condition of the exterior yet. Not in daylight anyway. There's probably more work out there."

"Well, I want to help with everything, Mom. I think this place is totally awesome—even just like this. But it would be cool to make it even better." He went for his second sandwich. "I can't believe it's really ours. Our very own house—and it comes with a great big ocean!"

Again, she felt the guilt . . . but didn't want to burst his bubble. Not yet. "It was incredibly generous of Poppa to leave it to us." She lifted her tea mug up like a toast. "Thank you, Poppa," she said reverently. "And Gammi too."

"Yes," Jackson echoed, clicking his glass against the mug. "Thank you, Poppa and Gammi. We'll take really, really good care of it." He downed the remains of his milk, then wiped his mouth with the back of his hand.

"I wish you'd had a chance to know them." Wendy stood to clear the table.

"I feel like I *do* know them." Jackson hopped up to help. "Or like I'm *getting* to know them. Just being here in this house—it's like I can feel them here. Not like ghosts or anything weird or scary. But like we're part of their family. It's pretty cool, Mom."

"You know, I can feel them too." She rinsed a plate, feeling a mixture of sadness and comfort washing over her. "And I know they're both really happy that we're here." She smiled at her son.

"Where's the dishwasher?" Jackson asked.

"You're looking at 'em." She pointed to him and then herself.

He laughed. "Okay then."

"But I'll handle it tonight. You go finish unpacking and make up your bed with some fresh sheets. They should be in the laundry basket you just brought in."

"Want me to put more wood on the fire first?" he called from the living room.

"Yes, please! The wood-box is just outside the—"

"I already saw it, Mom."

As she washed a turquoise dinner plate, she knew that some things, including these colorful Fiestaware dishes, would be going home to Cincinnati with them. Then, seeing that everything in the kitchen cupboards was coated with dust and grime, she decided to start washing everything. Poppa had never been much good at housekeeping, and guessing by the supply of paper plates and Styrofoam cups, he'd probably lived a fairly spartan life here at the cottage.

As she emptied the packed cupboards, she decided to do some thinning too, boxing up old worn items she wouldn't want to take home or even use while here. She was just getting the dishes replaced in the freshly cleaned cabinets when Jackson returned.

"I got my stuff all put away, and I put the box with your things in that spare room," he told her. "What's next?"

She closed the last cupboard door. "I still need to unpack and change sheets . . . and do some sorting in the downstairs bedroom. You can just relax if you want."

"I turned on that old TV," Jackson said, "but it doesn't get anything."

"No, they never had cable. It was just for watching movies," she explained. "Not that we ever did much of that, but Gammi had some old VHS movies."

"Movies on tape?"

She nodded. "Definitely old-school."

"Cool."

"And did you see Poppa's record player in the living room?"

"Like for vinyl?" Jackson's eyes lit up.

"Yeah, it's that massive wooden cabinet beneath the front window. It has an old turntable inside, as well as a radio. Poppa liked his music. He kept his vinyl records inside the stereo cabinet. I'll bet they're still there."

"Epic cool. Can I play one of them now? I mean, if they're there. Do you mind?"

"Not at all." She ruffled his thick dark hair. "You're an old-soul man, Jackson. Your great-grandpa would be proud."

"Well, wasn't I named for him?"

She nodded. "Yep. Jackson was his last name."

As she turned off the kitchen lights, she could hear strains of Dean Martin wafting through the cottage, so warm and cheerful and inviting . . . She almost expected to see Poppa and Gammi dancing past her, like they sometimes did on a warm summer evening after sharing a bottle of red wine and a good seafood dinner.

"That's nice," she told Jackson as she carried the laundry basket of linens into the downstairs bedroom. "Friendly."

"I thought you'd like it." He perused the albums, setting a few aside.

"After I get the bedroom cleared out a little and some clean sheets on, I could make us some popcorn," she offered. "You know, to celebrate our first night here."

"Sounds awesome." He nodded.

Bracing herself for an onslaught of old memories, she was pleasantly surprised to discover her grandparents' personal belongings had been completely cleared out of their bedroom. Only the bed and mattress, some sparse furnishings, and an attractive selection of shells remained. Was this the work of Mrs. Campbell? Or had Poppa done it? Mrs. Campbell had mentioned that he'd acted like he was getting the place ready for her. She wasn't sure about that, but it was a relief not to sift through clothes and shoes and miscellaneous toiletries.

It didn't take long to make up the bed and unpack her clothes. She was glad that she'd brought her own freshly laundered bedding from home. It would be a comfort to sleep on sweet-smelling sheets. Even though this had once been her grandparents' room, she was surprised by how at home she felt after her things were put in place.

"All done." She sniffed as she emerged from the bedroom, spying Jackson with his hands behind his back and a mysterious grin. "Did *you* make popcorn?"

He pulled a large bowl from behind him. "I found a hot-air popper."

"Good for you." She reached for a buttery handful. "Yum."

"I also found a case of root beer on the back porch." He sheepishly pointed to a couple of cans on the coffee table. "I know you're not a fan of soda, but since we're celebrating, I thought it'd be okay."

"Sounds good to me." She chuckled. "You know, root beer was Poppa's favorite."

So with the fire crackling and Dean Martin crooning in the background, she and Jackson feasted on popcorn and root beer—and for a brief moment Wendy could almost imagine living like this . . . *always.*

"This place is going to be so great at Christmastime." Jackson laid another log on the fire. "So much better than our cheesy apartment." He pointed to the big front window that looked toward the ocean. "I think we should put our Christmas tree right there."

Wendy pursed her lips.

"Or maybe over there." He pointed to the adjacent wall. "So we don't block the ocean view. And we can't get a little fake tree like last year. We'll get a real tree from now on. One that reaches clear to the ceiling too. I'll bet Maine has a great selection of Christmas trees."

She set down her root beer, trying to think of a response—a way to subdue his newfound holiday enthusiasm. "Well, maybe we should focus on Thanksgiving first. After all, it's just a few days away." And so they talked about that some, discussing what they'd cook and who would do what until Wendy eventually noticed the time. "Wow, Jackson, it's after ten. I don't know about you, but I'm exhausted. I think I'll turn in. I'd say you should too, but since it's not a school night—"

"I wanna go to bed," he agreed. "According to my phone, the low tide is at 5:12 tomorrow morning. That's supposed to be the best time for beachcombing."

She frowned. "Sorry, but I don't plan to be up by then. Besides, it'll still be dark."

"I know. The sunrise isn't until after seven. Maybe we could go then."

"Great. It's a date." She went over to kiss his forehead. "Good night, Jackson. Thanks for all your help with everything."

"Do we need to do anything about the fireplace?" he asked.

"I'll just make sure the logs are pushed back." She remembered how Poppa would do that. "And secure the fire screen in place."

"All right." He nodded. "G'night, Mom."

Wendy felt slightly odd as she went about locking up the house, turning off the lights, checking the fireplace. Obviously, she'd been a "grown-up" for many years, but her last time here, she'd been the kid and her grandparents took care of such things. Finally, with only the orange glow of the fireplace embers for light, she stood in the center of the cozy room. Looking around, she released a slow, long sigh that was partly relief and partly frustration.

In a "perfect" world, she and Jackson could just remain here and make this cottage their home sweet home. In a "perfect" world she could find profitable employment in

Seaside—year-round. But she knew there was no such thing as a perfect world. And she knew that not only did tiny Seaside lack corporate jobs in marketing firms like where she'd been employed these past seven years, the off-season was slim pickings for locals too. Jackson wasn't the only one doing research. She'd scoured the local newspaper's classified section online, as well as some job websites, only to learn it was hopeless.

As the head of her household and a responsible parent, Wendy needed a secure family-wage job that included insurance, vacation time, retirement benefits—a job that would help get them ahead and build up Jackson's college fund. And that job did not exist in Seaside.

These were the hard facts of life, but not information she was ready to dispense to her optimistic son . . . not yet. In the case of their Seaside visit, what he did not know would not hurt him. Let him enjoy a blissful break for another week or so. The harsh wakeup call of cold reality would come soon enough. She had no choice—the beach cottage had to be sold. And despite Jackson's dreams of Christmas by the sea, they would be long gone by then.

# Four

WENDY FELT strangely energized the next morning, waking up even before the sun rose. She couldn't remember when she'd slept so soundly. It was partly the result of exhaustion from the long days of driving and lousy nights in roadside motels, but it was also due to the ocean's surf. She'd always loved the comforting sound that used to lull her to sleep as a child—so much so that she often slept with her bedroom window open so she could hear it even better. Of course, that had been in the summertime. No one in their right mind would want windows open right now.

She shivered as she turned on the bedroom wall heater. Then, with bare feet, she hurried to the living room, cranking that heater up too. Poppa's insulation efforts and the installation of several wall heaters helped, but the cottage didn't have central heating—and she'd forgotten Mrs. Campbell's reminder to turn the heaters back on last night.

She was soon dressed and making a pot of coffee. She smiled as she poured water into the coffee maker—the same machine she'd sent Poppa for Christmas nearly fifteen years ago. It had been a duplicate wedding gift, but knowing how much Poppa loved a good cup of coffee, she knew he'd appreciate the regift. And judging by the brown-stained carafe—before she scrubbed it out—it'd been well used.

She was just cracking eggs into a bowl when Jackson came into the kitchen. Completely dressed, he looked bright and cheerful. "Want me to make another fire to warm it up some?" he asked.

She tried not to look overly doubtful. "Think you know how?"

"Yeah, I just did some research. It looks easy."

"Great. I forgot to turn the heaters on before we went to bed. I hope you didn't get too cold."

"Nah, I was fine. It's a lot warmer up there than down here."

She nodded, remembering that heat rises. "We'll have to check the wood supply today. There's a woodshed out back, but I'm not sure Poppa kept it stocked in recent years. We might need to pace ourselves with our fires."

By the time breakfast was ready, Jackson had a small fire going. "I'm impressed," she told him as they sat next to it to eat. "I had no idea you were such a Boy Scout."

"I just did like I saw on YouTube. The trick is dry fuel and good air flow." He explained the process in detail. "And I looked inside the woodshed, Mom. It was pretty full."

"Great. We'll have a fire every night."

"Won't we want to ration it some—to make it all the way through winter?"

She pursed her lips. As much as she hated to rain on his parade, she didn't want him being deluded. "I never promised we'd stay here all winter, Jackson. You know that I need—"

"But you didn't know how great it would be here. You were being all Negative Nellie. This place is awesome."

"Yes, but we have to—"

"Come on, Mom. Let's just enjoy it, okay?" His expression was so hopeful that she couldn't bear to set him straight. If Jackson wanted to live in denial for a while, why spoil it with an argument? Reality would come soon enough. Why not enjoy the moment while it lasted?

"It's a nice clear day," Jackson said as they finished eating. "But it's pretty chilly out there."

"Still want to go beachcombing?" she asked as they carried their dishes to the kitchen.

"Absolutely." He set his plate in the sink. "Is it all right if I do these dishes when we get back? I know it's my turn."

"That's fine. I'll get my coat and my phone. It's too early to call a handyman now, but I can call from down there."

"Do you think it's okay if I wear the boots I found on the back porch? They look like my size."

"They must've been Poppa's. I'm sure he'd love for you to have them."

Before long, they were out on the beach with their gathering buckets. It was nearly nine when she called Mrs. Campbell's handyman Gordon, but she was able only to leave a message. They walked for another hour or so, but found only a handful of shells—and nothing very impressive. "Shell finding is always better after a storm," she told Jackson as they paused to look out over the water. "It was one reason I never minded when we had a summer storm."

"Is that how your grandparents found all their cool stuff?"

"I'm sure storms helped, but it was also their daily diligence to—" She paused when she heard her phone jingling. "That's probably the handyman." She eagerly answered.

"I got your message, Mrs. Harper," Gordon said in a slow Maine drawl. "I can come on out there first thing this morning if you like."

"That'd be great." She briefly described the condition of the bathroom floor.

"Sounds like you got yourself some dry rot all right. Best to get onto that before it gets worse. The Millers out your way let their problem go too long and next thing you know they got termites. You ain't seen no sign of termites, have you?"

"No, no, I don't think so."

"Well, you never know."

"When can you come out?" she asked.

"Lemme finish my coffee, and I'm on my way."

"Great. My son and I are on the beach right now, but we'll hurry back. And if we're not there, just go inside. The back door's unlocked." She told him goodbye and pocketed her phone. "He's coming," she told Jackson. "That means I need to get back ASAP. You can keep shell hunting if you like but I'll—"

"Nah, I'll go back with you. Did you really leave the door unlocked, Mom?" He looked concerned.

"This is Seaside. My grandparents never locked up. No one did." She smiled nervously. Hopefully that was still the practice. "Mind if we jog back? I'd like to be there when Gordon arrives."

Wendy was relieved to make it home before the handyman. "I want to clear everything out of the bathroom," she told Jackson. "Makes it easier for Gordon—and the less time it takes him, the better it'll be for our budget."

"Maybe he'll let me help him," Jackson offered. "That might save some time."

Wendy nodded. "Good idea." She started emptying the linen cabinet, and with Jackson's help they soon got the old-fashioned bathroom completely cleared out. For a long moment, she studied the space. It was actually a good-sized bathroom. Bigger than the one in their apartment, it had a claw-foot tub and an acrylic shower that her grandparents had gotten installed when she was about Jackson's age. Hopefully the dry rot wasn't too bad. It would be expensive to have it all redone.

"Hallo the house," a deep voice called.

"In here," she yelled back.

A short, balding man introduced himself as Gordon and immediately started poking around the floor with a screwdriver, actually puncturing a hole right through the linoleum. "You definitely got yourself some dry rot here. Probably a leaky toilet seal." He looked up at her. "I gotta pull the toilet and, unless I'm wrong, most of the underlayment too. Means you'll be without your bathroom awhile. You got another one?"

"No, this is it." She frowned.

"You got another place to stay? Friends nearby?"

"No," she said firmly. "How long will it take to repair it?"

He rubbed his chin. "Well, if the dry rot is just 'neath the toilet, I suppose I could be done in a day or two—maybe three or four if it's worse."

"I can help you," Jackson offered.

Gordon nodded. "Might speed things along some to have a helper."

Wendy wanted to ask how much this was going to cost,

but she knew it was pointless. It had to be done. Still, what would they do without a usable bathroom?

"So you want me to start tearing it out now?" Gordon stood up, hooking his thumbs into his bright yellow suspenders. "It'll be a mess."

"But it has to be done?"

"Yep." He dipped his bristly chin.

"Then I'd appreciate it if you could start right away."

"Will do." He pocketed his screwdriver. "And if I were you, I'd run into the hardware store and pick myself up a camp toilet. To get you by until I'm done in here."

"Okay." She nodded. "Anything else I need?"

"Well, you're gonna need some new flooring."

"Flooring?"

"To replace that linoleum. The hardware store don't got a lot to choose from, but if you're not too picky, you might find something that'll do. Otherwise you gotta drive yourself over to Portland to one of them *big box* stores."

"Okay." Wendy did not want to drive to Portland.

He looked around the bathroom. "Your fixtures look to be in good shape. Shouldn't need to replace anything. Well, unless you're wanting fancy updates."

"No," she said quickly. "I like the old-fashioned look in here."

He tapped a shower wall. "Sure hope that dry rot don't go clear behind here. Hate to have to tear this out." He bent down and poked with his screwdriver again.

She frowned. "How does it look?"

"Hard to say." He stood. "Gotta open it up to find out." He turned to Jackson. "Wanna help me get some tools and things from my truck?"

"Sure." Jackson nodded.

"I guess I'll go to the hardware store," Wendy said. "Jackson, I've got my phone. If anything comes up, you just call me, okay?"

"Sure." He paused from following Gordon. "Are you okay, Mom?"

"Okay?" She smiled stiffly. "Yeah, sure, of course."

"Are you worried about money?" he persisted.

She shrugged. "Well, I hadn't really planned on these kinds of expenses."

"Remember how you always used to say that God takes care of us," he reminded her. "You and Dad used to tell me God will provide what we need."

"You're right, Jackson." She sighed. From the mouths of babes . . . or preadolescents. "Thanks."

"So maybe we just need to trust him more."

Her smile grew more genuine. "I'll try to keep that in mind."

As she drove to town, Wendy pondered Jackson's reminder. Didn't she used to trust God to provide? She and Edward had both believed that God would meet all their needs. When had she quit? Was it when Edward got sick? Or when they paid more than they had saved for medical treatment that didn't work? Or after he was gone and all the bills kept pouring in? She wasn't even sure, but she knew that Jackson was right—she had forgotten. She wasn't even sure she believed it anymore. For Jackson's sake, she wanted to believe it. But in light of life these past few years . . . well, it felt impossible.

Driving through town, she marveled at the many improvements. From the sidewalk pavers to charming streetlamps to the variety of businesses, the village looked bigger and better than ever. Even the city park looked clean and fresh, with sturdy benches and inviting picnic tables. She parked across the street from the hardware store, noticing that several shops and a couple of restaurants appeared to be open. Seaside was not nearly as dead as she'd imagined it would be during the off-season.

Noticing a big plush turkey in the toy-store window, she remembered this was Thanksgiving week. Perhaps that was why the town felt lively. Maybe tourists were here for the holiday week. Next to the toy store was one of her favorite shops, She Sells Sea Shells. Wendy was glad to see it was still in business. Someday she'd have to take Jackson in there. Next to the shell shop was an elegant-looking furniture store called Driftwood. That was new. She peered in the window to see some gorgeous pieces of expensive-looking furniture. If money were no object, she'd love to get some of those pieces for the beach cottage. Unfortunately, that was not going to happen.

Wendy breathed deeply as she crossed the street at the corner. The sea air was incredibly energizing. So clean and fresh and invigorating. Even the fishy smell wafting in from the docks didn't bother her. It never had. The hardware store looked pretty much the same as she recalled. At least on the outside. When she wheeled a cart through, she could see that it had been modernized and was much better stocked than she remembered. The good signage helped her quickly find the camping aisle. Hopefully Gordon was right about finding a portable camp toilet here, but the more she looked, the less hopeful she felt. Was there really such a thing?

"Need some help?"

She glanced up to see a tall man with dark wavy hair. Dressed casually in faded blue jeans and a plaid flannel shirt, he appeared to be carefully checking her out. He likely suspected she wasn't a local. Hardware store employees were probably familiar with everyone in this small town. "I'm looking for, uh, a temporary toilet," she said with a bit of embarrassment. "You know, the kind they take camping. Do you have anything like that?"

His dark brows arched with amusement. "Going camping this time of year?"

"No." She hid her irritation at his freshness. "Our bathroom is being torn out and we need something to—"

"Oh, yeah, I get it." He nodded. "But if you're under construction, you should consider getting an outhouse so that your workers—"

"That's not necessary," she declared. "The project should only take a day or two."

"Okay." He slowly led her to the end of the aisle. "Looks like a couple of options right here." He pointed to some boxes. "Now, if it were me, I'd go with this model." He tapped the biggest box. "Looks sturdier. Not that you'd need a particularly hefty potty yourself." He chuckled like this was highly amusing, and she could tell by the way he was talking that he actually knew nothing about the products he was attempting to sell her. Wendy couldn't believe she was standing here discussing toilets with a perfect stranger. Not that he was perfect—although he *was* rather attractive. But she didn't appreciate him making fun of her—and he was obviously enjoying her discomfort a bit too much. Maybe he'd forgotten to study the customer service section in his employees' manual.

"Fine," she retorted. "I'll take that one."

He reached down to pick it up. "It's a little big for your cart. How about I take it up front for you?"

"Thank you," she said crisply.

He eased the bulky box from the shelf and onto the floor, leaning it against his leg. "So . . . you're new in town?"

"Not exactly." She watched as he easily picked up the container. Was he trying to be friendly or actually hitting on her—and did it even matter?

He hoisted the carton to his shoulder. "But you're not a tourist, are you?"

"Not exactly," she repeated her intentionally vague answer.

"But you are remodeling your bathroom." He grinned. "Anything else I can help you with? Need a sink or a—"

"I do need some flooring," she admitted. "Although I've heard your selection is limited."

He pointed toward the back of the store. "That's the building section back there. I think flooring is on aisle 22 or 23, but I wouldn't stake my life on it."

"Thank you." She turned away from him, rolling her eyes and her cart—trying to get away from this weird employee and wondering why she felt so irked at him. After all, he was trying to be helpful and he was awfully good-looking. But it was his offhanded teasing that had gotten under her skin. Besides that, he was too nosy. What business was it of his to know her status in Seaside? She turned onto aisle 22 and was pleasantly surprised to find several flooring options. Some big rolls of vinyl as well as packages of tile squares. Unfortunately, she'd forgotten to measure. So she pulled out her phone and called Jackson, asking him to find out.

"It's seven feet wide . . . and almost ten feet long," he informed her just as the obnoxious sales guy returned.

"How's the project going?" she asked Jackson, trying to appear preoccupied so the salesman would go away and mind his own business.

"Great, Mom. Gordon's already got the toilet removed. I carried it outside for him. It was pretty heavy, but I got it by myself."

"Good. I should be home—"

"Gotta go, Mom. Gordon is calling."

She pocketed her phone, turning her attention to the three choices of roll-out vinyl. One was dark and dreary, one was faux wood, and one resembled white tiles.

"Find anything you like?" the salesman asked.

She frowned. "Not particularly. But I suppose that would work." She pointed to the shiny white one. "Although I don't really like it and I'm not sure it's wide enough."

"Says it's 72 inches wide." He pointed to the sign next to the rack. "That'd be six feet."

"I can do the math." She refrained from rolling her eyes again.

"How big is your bathroom?"

She repeated what Jackson had just told her.

"That's not going to work for you. Not without a seam, and no one wants a seam in a bathroom. If they can help it."

"Oh, yeah." She conceded. "Well, it's kind of cheap looking anyway."

He pursed his lips then nodded. "Gotta agree with you there." He pointed to the boxed tiles. "What about these stick-on tiles? You got your faux travertine, faux granite, and then you got the solid colors—white, gray, and black."

She frowned, trying to imagine any of these options in the old-fashioned bathroom. None of it seemed quite right. Maybe she was in over her head.

He picked up a black square in one hand and a white one in the other. "I used these to make a checkerboard pattern in a small bathroom, and if I do say so myself, it turned out pretty nice. They're easy for a do-it-yourselfer, and these stick-on tiles are surprisingly tough. For the money, you can't beat 'em."

Like a lightbulb going on, she instantly envisioned a charming black-and-white checkerboard floor in the cottage bathroom—it would look sweet with the old-fashioned white sink and claw-foot tub. And perhaps she could put some accent color on the wall. It all made sense. Her eyes moved from the two squares still in his hands up to the smiling face of the man holding them. In that same instant she felt a strange little jolt inside of her. As if a dormant part of her had just been poked and awakened . . . almost like coming to life. And although it was a pleasant sensation, it was somewhat unsettling.

# Five

I THINK YOU SOLD ME on it," Wendy declared. "Checkerboard it is."

"Really? You like it?" His eyes lit up, and she realized they were a deep shade of blue—slightly out of place with his dark brown hair, and yet strikingly attractive.

"And you're not exaggerating? Is installation really easy?" She took a square from him, carefully examining both sides, testing it for strength and trying not to think about those deep blue eyes.

"It's easy-breezy. As long as you have a smooth, flat, and very clean surface."

She pursed her lips. "And you really think I can do it?"

He appeared to size her up, then grinned. "You look fit to me. I'm sure you can handle it."

She flushed slightly as she bent down to pick up a box of tiles. Was he flirting?

"Here," he said quickly. "Let me get these for you. The boxes are heavier than they look." He set a box of white tiles followed by a black one into her cart. "There you go."

"Is that enough?"

His mouth twisted to one side. "Probably more than

enough, but it's better to have too many than not enough, and the store will let you return what you don't use."

"Thanks." She smiled, trying to act perfectly natural. "You've been very helpful."

"Glad to be of service. Anything else I can help you with? Need any towel racks or bathroom accessories while you're in home-improvement mode?"

She considered this. If she wanted the cottage to show nicely, it might be wise to replace the flimsy old towel bars and hooks and things after all. "Come to think of it, that's not a bad idea."

"Right this way." He led her down another aisle and then another. "I, uh, think we're getting closer."

Eventually they found a decent selection, but Wendy couldn't decide on the finish. "I kind of like the bronze," she said. "But I'm not sure that's best."

"What metal are your plumbing fixtures?"

"Chrome."

"Maybe you should match them."

She nodded. "Yes, you're absolutely right."

She loaded several pieces in her cart. Then feeling dis-combobulated, she aimed her cart for the front of the store. But the salesman stayed with her, chatting pleasantly all the way, then pausing by the paint section. "Need any paint?" he asked hopefully.

"As a matter of fact." She glanced over the multitude of cans with uncertainty. "Can you help me with that too?"

"Sure. Is this for the bathroom as well?"

"Actually, I plan to paint just about everything in the cot-tage," she told him. "I mean, as far as the interior goes. Hope-fully the exterior is okay."

"Do you have any specific colors in mind?"

"I should probably keep most of the walls neutral," she said. "Something light and bright, but not too stark. Some pleasant shade of white."

He went straight to the rack of paint samples like he knew what he was doing. "This has a nice selection of white shades." He handed her a pamphlet. "And it's a good-quality paint company." He pointed to a shade called White Sand. "This one is nice."

She studied the color, holding it up to the light coming in from the front door. "I like it," she agreed. "Clean and fresh, but not too bright or stark. Kind of beachy too. Good choice."

"Great." He waved to another employee. "Hey, Allan," he called out. "How about mixing us some paint over here?"

Allan asked Wendy a few questions, then went to work mixing a five-gallon bucket of White Sand paint.

She turned back to the original salesman, wondering why he wasn't wearing a name badge like Allan. She was curious as to his name, but didn't want to show her interest by asking. "I'd like to get a couple of colors," she told him. "The bathroom could use something to perk it up. It's got beadboard wainscot that I could paint the White Sand color, but it would be fun to have something different on the wall above. I'd like it to look beachy too. Maybe a blue or green shade, you know, like the sea. Do you think that would look nice with the checkerboard?"

"I can see that." He led her over to a section of colors, then quickly selected a very pale turquoise blue, holding it up. "How about this? It's called Sea Glass."

She stared at the color, which really did remind her of sea

52

glass, then looked up at him in wonder. "That's perfect," she admitted. "You're really good at this."

"Thanks." He grinned. "Anything else I can help you with?"

"Well, I'd like to paint the kitchen cabinets too. I'm not sure what color exactly, but I'd like something to perk up the kitchen. The countertops are just white laminate, and I don't plan to replace them. And the floors, well, they'll probably need to be redone too."

"So . . . this a small house?" he asked with interest. "Like a beach cottage perhaps?"

"How'd you guess?"

He shrugged. "It's not a big leap in these parts. Anyway, since it's a small house you might not want to get too many colors going—might feel too busy."

"Tell me the truth." She narrowed her eyes. "Are you an interior decorator?" she teased.

"Nope." He laughed as he pulled out another color sample. "But how about this for your cabinets? It's kind of bold, but might be fun in a small kitchen. And it's beachy."

She studied the slightly darker shade of turquoise blue. "I actually think that would be really nice." She could imagine it with the Fiestaware dishes—it would make a real statement in the drab, tired kitchen.

He fanned out the three paint samples for her approval. "They go nicely together. Good for a small house."

"I love it," she told him. "I don't know how you picked them so easily."

"I've been told I have a good eye." He handed the two blue samples to Allan, explaining what they were for. "A quart should be plenty for the cabinets and probably a gallon for the pale blue, although she'll probably only need half of it."

While Allan mixed, the first salesman helped her to pick out some painting tools. The whole time he continued making small talk with her. He was clearly intent on extracting some information. Grateful for his assistance, she no longer felt irked at his curiosity. Without disclosing everything, she explained about summers spent in Seaside and how she was now fixing up a beach cottage that she'd inherited.

"I don't have much time to get a lot done." She set a paint tray and roller on top of the other items.

"What's the hurry?"

"Well, I have to get it done in order to . . . well, before Christmas."

"So do you have anyone around to help you with your improvements?"

She suspected he wanted to know if she had a significant other. Instead she told him about Gordon the handyman.

"Oh, yeah, Gordon is the best. Good for you."

"And I've got my son, Jackson. He's only twelve, but he's extremely helpful."

He appeared to consider this, but to her relief, didn't push anymore. "I seem to have forgotten my manners." He stuck out his hand. "My name is Caleb Colton. I've lived in Seaside my whole life. Well, aside from college and a few years in the Big Apple, where I thought I was going to find a more interesting life." He shook his head. "I was wrong about that."

"Oh . . ." She nodded as they shook hands. "I'm Wendy Harper."

"Welcome to Seaside," he said. "Or maybe I should say welcome *back*."

She studied him closely, wondering. "Do you think our paths might've crossed as kids . . . I mean, here in Seaside?"

"I wouldn't be surprised." His smile was lopsided. "But you probably wouldn't recognize me or remember me from back then. I was a pretty geeky teen. Scrawny with braces. Seriously, I could pass for twelve when I was sixteen. Not a real chick magnet." He chuckled.

Wendy stopped herself from admitting that he'd grown up rather nicely. Just then, Allan announced that her paint was ready. Caleb appeared determined to continue helping, loading the smaller buckets in her cart and carrying the biggest one to the cash register, waiting as the cashier rang it up. Wendy tried not to look as shocked as she felt by the total, swallowing hard as she handed over her credit card. *This is an investment,* she told herself as she signed her name. *I'll pay it all back with the sale of the house.* Hopefully soon!

"I'll help you get it to your car." Caleb picked up the big paint bucket and the toilet box.

Still feeling stunned—and a bit light-headed—she followed him out, waiting as Caleb loaded everything into the back of her Subaru. "Thank you so much," she told him. "I really appreciate it. I didn't know the hardware store had such great customer service."

He laughed as he closed the back of the car then turned to face her. "So . . . you say you'll be without plumbing for a few days?"

"Gordon said a couple days—more if the damage is bad."

"Do you have plans for Thanksgiving? If you don't have plumbing by then, you probably can't cook much."

"I haven't really thought about that." She shrugged, adjusting the strap of her bag. "I guess Jackson and I will go out for dinner to celebrate." She smiled brightly as she opened the driver's side door. "Thanks again, Caleb." Without giving him a chance to pursue this further, she hopped into the car, gave a cheery wave, then backed out.

Wendy wasn't sure why she felt so unsettled as she drove back home. It wasn't as if Caleb had done anything wrong. Sure, he'd teased her some, but it was probably just his personality, simply being small-town friendly. Albeit a bit too friendly for her taste. But she didn't want to get involved with a guy right now. Not because she was opposed to dating, per se. She'd actually let Claire set her up on a couple of blind dates this past year. Disastrous dates, as it had turned out. But her real reason to hold an attractive, friendly fellow like Caleb Colton at arm's length was simply because she and Jackson were only here *temporarily*. There was no point in encouraging a connection.

Still, unless she was imagining things, Caleb had been about to invite her to Thanksgiving. How weird would that have been? Sharing a traditional family holiday with someone you barely know? Well, maybe it was sweet, but it was also unsettling. Really, she'd prefer eating at a restaurant with Jackson . . . just like they'd done these last few years . . . since losing Edward. Stark? Maybe. But it had become their tradition.

And it wasn't that she never got gracious invitations to join friends or coworkers on holidays. Claire and Rich always wanted her and Jackson to join them—for any occasion. Although Wendy tried to think she'd accept someday, in the meantime she preferred to avoid gatherings with intact families simply because it made her sad. Of course, it was somewhat selfish and not something she could easily admit to. Not even to Jackson. And certainly not to a stranger—even a handsome and helpful one like Caleb Colton. Really, what would be the point of furthering a pointless acquaintance?

Wendy was not prepared for the chaos she found when she arrived at the cottage. Although Gordon's truck was gone, the toilet, bathtub, and sink were scattered in front of the house, along with an ugly pile of nasty-looking wood and torn-up linoleum debris. Like a real junkyard. Hopefully the neighbors wouldn't complain.

The inside of the cottage was no better. Welcomed with a mess of dirty footsteps on the kitchen floor, she picked her way past tools and junk and a couple buckets of water. She wanted to protest, but knew this was all simply necessary. Still, as she walked through what felt like an invaded space, she wished she could afford to put herself and Jackson in the hotel down the street until the repairs were wrapped up. Even though she could rationalize that the hotel expense would be repaid by the sale of the cottage, she still needed to protect her credit card's limit for the duration of this rehab phase. She needed to remember there was no guarantee she would sell the house . . . and then what?

"How's it going?" she asked Jackson.

"Gordon says it's going to take *several* days."

She grimaced as she set a paint bucket on the kitchen table. "Is the shower going to be okay?"

"He thinks the dry rot didn't go that far. But most of the bathroom floor had to be completely torn out. He even has to replace the floor joists."

"Floor joists?" That sounded expensive.

"That's these big pieces of wood that hold up the whole bathroom floor. The old ones were rotted right through.

Gordon went to the lumberyard to get some new ones, but he said he won't be back until tomorrow."

"Tomorrow?" She frowned. "Do we have water in the meantime?"

"Nope, it's turned off." He pointed to the bucket of water on the floor. "I got those from Mrs. Campbell. She said we can use her hose as much as we need." He grinned. "It'll be kinda like camping, huh, Mom?"

"I guess so. Speaking of camping, our new toilet is in the back of the car."

"I'll get it," he offered.

"Why does the water have to be turned off if Gordon's not working on it right now?" she asked as she followed Jackson out to the car.

"Because the bathroom pipes are old and rotten—that's the reason there was a leak. So Gordon called a plumber to come look at it. He's supposed to come by sometime this afternoon."

She cringed inwardly. This was sounding more and more costly!

Jackson pointed to the five-gallon bucket in the back of the car. "Is that paint?"

"Yes. As long as the cottage is a mess, I might as well start painting."

"Can I help?" he asked.

"Absolutely. I haven't painted anything since before you were born. I painted our kitchen and your nursery, but as I recall, it's pretty hard work."

"Maybe I should do some research on YouTube," he said as he carried the toilet box into the house. "You know, to learn some painting tips."

"Great idea. I'm glad you're such a researcher. We'll knock this out in no time." Wendy wanted to maintain a brave front for Jackson's sake. He didn't need to worry about finances—although she knew the bathroom project was going to cost far more than she'd expected—that was her job. Anyway, the best plan was just to plunge ahead and get this place fixed up and hope for a quick sale. As she changed into painting clothes, she remembered what Jackson had said—reminding her that God would provide. She sure hoped her son's faith wouldn't be shaken if God did not provide—or not in the way that Jackson was hoping for. In the meantime, she would attempt to conjure up some faith of her own . . . but it wasn't going to be easy.

# Six

B Y WEDNESDAY AFTERNOON, Wendy had made a fair amount of painting progress. And she'd come up with an idea—something to address some of her financial woes. She'd been highly motivated to think of solutions after the plumber handed her an enormous bill for just nine hours of labor, plus materials. Who knew plumbers were so expensive? "Maybe you should consider becoming a plumber," she'd teased Jackson after going over the bill.

At least the water was back on—that was something. Unfortunately, the bathroom—aside from the shower—was still unusable. Gordon promised to have the fixtures back in by Saturday afternoon. "That's if you get your flooring installed by then," he'd told her after she showed him the tiles she'd chosen. "No sense getting your fixtures in if your floors aren't down. But you and Jackson oughta be able to lay these just fine." He gave her some pointers and even left her a couple of cutting tools.

Wendy had paid Gordon for what he'd already done, taking her meager checking account down even more. She had no idea how much his final bill would be or what other expenses lurked ahead, but as she painted in the living room, she'd been racking her brain for money-making ideas. Late last night, she'd even perused the storage room in hopes of unearthing some priceless antique or collectible she might be able to sell on eBay for a small fortune. Unfortunately, it was mostly junk. Interesting junk, but probably not highly valuable. Her best hope was probably getting this cottage ready to sell—ASAP. Even if a quick sale cut their "vacation" short, she didn't think she had any other options. Hopefully Jackson would understand.

So she'd thrown herself wholeheartedly into painting—working until nearly midnight last night and getting up at the crack of dawn to continue today. While preparing the most cluttered area of the living room for painting this morning, she'd boxed up hundreds of shells, driftwood bits, sea glass, and various treasures. Although she planned to keep some pieces, she knew there was far too much for their little apartment in Ohio. But she also knew these items had value. Tourist shops sold tons of this stuff in the height of the season. How many times had she prowled the shelves and aisles of She Sells Sea Shells when she was a child? And her favorite shell shop was still in business—the perfect place to sell some of these shells. For all she knew they could be worth hundreds of dollars. Maybe a couple thousand. Perhaps enough to cover the rest of the repairs for the cottage—as well as buy them some time. It really would be fun to remain here a few weeks.

Since she had to drive to town to pay her bill at the plumber's office, she decided to take a sample box of really nice seashells with her. She would drop by the shell shop and see if she could interest the proprietors in adding these beauties to their inventory. She wasn't sure what the value of this one box of shells might be, but she hoped it might be a couple hundred dollars. Enough to keep her bank account from completely shriveling.

After paying her plumbing bill, she got out her box and headed down the street. Hopefully, since it was the day before Thanksgiving and the town looked fairly busy, the shell shop would be open. Catching a glimpse of her reflection in a shoe store window almost made her rethink this plan. What was she thinking? With her paint-splattered old clothes and a faded bandana wrapped around her hair, she looked like a bag lady. But seeing a young couple emerging from She Sells Sea Shells with a purchase in hand, she decided to swallow her pride and go for it. After all, it was just a tourist shop, and the state of her finances was dire.

To her surprise, the shop was much nicer than she remembered. Instead of the junky tourist trap that she'd adored as a child, it was actually quite elegant. Certainly, there were still shells and treasures sprinkled about, but they were artfully displayed in gleaming glass cases with expensive looking jewelry inside—all very high-end and beautiful.

"Can I help you?" An attractive blonde woman studied Wendy with arched brows—as if to ask, *Is the bag lady lost?*

"Well, I—I'm not sure." Feeling conspicuous and foolish, Wendy set her slightly worn box of seashells on the counter. "I haven't been in here for years," she confessed. "I thought it was still a touristy shell shop—and that perhaps you'd like to purchase some interesting shells." She looked down at the box. "I have quite an unusual collection here. Some very—"

"No, thank you," the woman said crisply. "We don't *buy*

shells here." She frowned at the box. "We're not *that kind* of business."

Wendy felt the insult, but decided to dig herself in deeper. "Do you know of any other place that might—"

"No, I can't think of anyone who *buys* shells." The woman folded her arms in front of her with a disgruntled expression. "I'm sorry, I can't help you."

"I'm sorry to have troubled you." Wendy picked up her box just as the bell on the door jingled, and she heard someone coming in. Now she really wanted to disappear—or just blend in with the walls. She'd been foolish to enter this shop—and looking like this!

"Hello," a male voice called from in front.

"Hey there," the blonde woman chirped, smiling brightly past Wendy. "I was hoping you'd stop by and say hello." Her tone turned flirtatious. "So, tell me, what're you up to today?"

"Not much. How's business?"

"It's okay, but I've been missing you, Caleb."

Wendy felt a jolt at the name Caleb. Was this *her* Caleb— the guy from the hardware store? And if so, how could she avoid being seen by him? Feeling like a trapped rabbit, she moved away from the counter, slipping behind a rotating card rack, pretending to be interested in the glossy seascape images as she slowly backed away.

"Wendy?" Caleb came straight to her, grinning triumphantly. "Hey, I thought that was you walking through town just a few minutes ago." His eyes twinkled with amusement. "And it looks like you've been painting."

She nodded mutely. Could this get any more embarrassing?

He pointed to a splotch of Sea Glass blue paint on her arm. "So how did this shade look in your bathroom?"

She smiled meekly. "Pretty great. But the floor's not down yet."

"And the White Sand color?" He pointed to her other arm.

"I only got two walls painted in the living room so far, but it looks nice. Very clean and fresh."

"What about this shade?" He pointed to a splotch on her shoulder. "I don't remember you getting that color."

"I actually mixed that color myself," she admitted. "I took the half-used can of Sea Glass that was left over from the bathroom and filled it with some White Sand paint to get this pale blue color. I used it to paint my bedroom."

"Clever." He nodded with approval.

"It turned out really soft and pretty."

He peered down at the cardboard box in her hands. "What's that you got there?"

"Seashells," she muttered with embarrassment. She felt like a child who'd been trying to peddle her wares—unsuccessfully.

"Yes, I can see those are shells. But where are they from? What are you doing with them?"

She lowered her voice, attempting to explain. "You see, I was clearing things out, you know, to paint. My grandparents have a ton of this stuff. I love it, but don't know what to do with all of it. I thought a tourist shop might want to buy some." She glanced around the fancy store. "I didn't realize this shop had changed so much over the years."

He nodded as he picked up an abalone shell. "Yeah. Not much like when we were kids, is it?" He turned to the woman still behind the counter. "So what did you tell her, Crystal?"

The snooty blonde held up her hands in a helpless gesture. "Just that we don't buy seashells."

Caleb frowned. "But that's not completely true."

"Well, we do buy them, but only from our suppliers," she explained. "I think that's what Ashley said."

Caleb nodded to Wendy. "Why can't Wendy be a supplier?"

"I don't know . . . I mean, I'd have to ask Ashley." Crystal frowned.

"Did you call her?"

"Well, no . . ."

"Why not?" Caleb demanded.

"She said she's busy today. Getting ready for Thanksgiving and—"

"Never mind." Caleb turned back to Wendy. "Come with me." Instead of leading her to the front door, he led her toward the back of the store.

"Where are we going?" Feeling awkward, Wendy glanced back at Crystal in time to see her frown intensifying. But Crystal didn't try to stop them.

Caleb opened a door. "Go ahead," he told her.

"But what about that woman—"

"It's okay," he assured her.

She continued on, going into what appeared to be a small storage room. Tidy shelves filled with stacked boxes and bags lined the walls. "I don't think we're supposed to be back here," she said nervously.

"Don't worry." He led her past a counter with packing materials.

"Where are you taking me?" she demanded as he opened another door.

"Come on," he urged, tugging her into a darkened space that smelled vaguely of fresh cut wood.

"What are you do—"

"Give me a minute and I'll explain." He flicked on a switch and the roomy space was illuminated with long strips of fluorescent lights. She looked around to see what appeared to be a well-equipped woodworking shop, complete with workbenches, fancy-looking tools, and stacks of miscellaneous shapes of wood. "What's this? Are we trespassing?"

He grinned, waving a hand. "*This* is my woodshop."

"*Your* woodshop?"

He led her to a heavy worktable and pulled out a stool. "Have a seat."

She started to protest, but curiosity took over, so she sat down.

"I'd like a better look at your shells." He sat across from her and, sliding her box across the table, immediately began to sort through them, actually identifying many of them by name. "Wow, there are some beauties in here, Wendy."

"How is this *your* woodshop?" She stared in wonder at the well-organized space. "I thought you worked at the hardware store."

"Well, not actually. Although I did work there one summer as a kid, about twenty years ago. I just wanted to help you yesterday. So I made myself useful." He held a conch shell up to the light, letting out a low whistle. "Nice."

"But what about—"

"You see, I run a furniture shop. It's called Driftwood," he explained. "And this is—"

"Driftwood?" she echoed. "I looked in the window yesterday—it's a beautiful store."

"Thank you." He smiled, then waved to the workbench and tools. "This is where I make the furniture."

"*You* make the furniture?"

"Well, not all of it. I do buy a few pieces—the kinds of things I have no interest in creating. Also, they help fluff it up a little. You know, so the place doesn't get too sparse. Especially in summer when it's really busy out there."

She nodded, taking all this in.

"Anyway, the shell shop next door used to be my grandma's," he explained. "Back when we were kids. Then my mom took it over—oh, almost twenty years ago. For whatever reason, she wanted to make it fancy. More uptown for deep-pocketed citified tourists. I wasn't too enthused about the idea, but I have to admit it turned out to be a pretty smart business move. She manages to stay open and turn a profit year-round."

"But she doesn't buy seashells." Wendy frowned down at her box.

"Crystal was wrong about that. And I have no doubt my mom would be interested in some of these. Except that she's in Florida for the winter." He picked up a large scallop shell, holding it up. "However, I might be interested in some of these."

"Really?" She frowned. "Are you just being nice?"

"Not at all." He stood, picking up the box. "I'm closed today, but come into my store and I'll show you around . . . if you like."

Within moments he was giving her a tour of what was an amazingly beautiful store. Not only were there gorgeous pieces of handmade wood furniture, but there were decorative items as well—items that had been crafted from arrangements of beautiful shells or nautical items. "I order these accessories from a catalogue." He pointed to a large mirror trimmed in spikes of driftwood and a lamp with a shade covered in shells. "These accent pieces, along with my furnishings, sell like hotcakes in the summertime." He went over to the counter, pulling out a shiny catalogue. "See." He flipped through the pages, showing her item after item. "These boxes are really popular." He pointed to a picture framed with scallop shells. "Each is one-of-a-kind. Not cheap either."

She nodded, studying the photograph closely. "I'll bet they're not that hard to make," she mused aloud. "Just a glue gun and a few supplies."

"Especially if you already have the raw materials," he pointed to her box of shells. "And if you have an artistic bent." He glanced curiously at her. "Do you?"

She turned to him in surprise. "I've dabbled in art some."

"I had a feeling."

"Why?" she asked. "What made you think that?"

"Just a hunch. The way you were dressed the other day . . . sort of 'boho-chic,' my sister would probably say. But I suspected as much."

"So, do you think if I made some of these pieces that I could sell them?"

"Sure. Maybe not so much in the wintertime. But you could get a good start—create a nice stockpile for summer."

"For summer . . ." She didn't want to admit that summer would be too late.

"The off-season is always slow. Oh, I'll probably get some traffic in here between Thanksgiving and Christmas, but after that, I usually just close shop. Unless it's a holiday weekend. But I don't mind. It gives me time to work uninterrupted and build up my stock for the busy season."

"Right." She slowly nodded, wondering if she could possibly create any pieces in time for Christmas shoppers. It didn't sound realistic. Not with everything else she had to accomplish before returning to Ohio. "Well, I don't want to take any more of your time." She closed the catalogue and picked up her box. "But I must admit that was interesting. Thanks for showing—"

"Wait," he said. "I was serious about wanting to buy your shells."

"Why?" she asked, studying his face and wishing he wasn't quite so handsome—or so nice.

"Sometimes I use shells for inlay on wood pieces. Besides, I like having them around for accents." He pointed to a table. "For instance, a basket of pretty shells would look great there, don't you think?" He pointed to a wall shelf. "Or a few up there, maybe with a candle or something."

She grinned. "I *knew* you were an interior decorator."

"Well, that's a bit of a stretch, but I suppose you weren't totally wrong." He shrugged. "And my mother likes to brag to her friends that I'm an *arteest*."

She ran a hand over the sleek golden top of a live-edge console table. "I'd have to agree with her. This is gorgeous."

"Thank you." He jerked his thumb toward the back room. "How about if you leave your box of shells with me? I'll go through them and come up with what I think is a fair price—that is, if you can trust me with them."

"Of course." She nodded. "That'd be fine."

"And I'll buy some for the shell shop too. Despite what Crystal says, I've got a feeling my mom and sis would be glad to get their hands on some of these beauties."

"Great."

He led her to the front door. "I'll let you out here—so you

won't have to cross paths with Crystal again. I'm sorry she was being so snooty. She's not usually like that."

"Maybe it was how I was dressed." Wendy laughed to see the paint still on her hands, wedged into her fingernails, and probably in her hair. "I probably scared her."

"So how is your plumbing project coming?" He opened the door. "You got running water yet?"

"Don't ask." She let out a groan as she went outside. "It's worse than we thought—but it should be done by the weekend."

"Well, I was trying to invite you and your son and, uh, anyone else in your family . . . I thought you might want to share Thanksgiving with me and my family." His tone was warm. "But you were giving me the brush-off."

She considered the state of the beach cottage as well as the expense of taking Jackson out for a fancy dinner—especially in light of her unfortunate finances. "You know, Caleb, that sounds really wonderful. We'd love to come. What can we bring?"

"Just bring yourselves and a pair of athletic shoes."

"Huh?"

"Hopefully you like to play football," he said, writing an address on a small pad. "Here." He tore it off and gave it to her. "Two o'clock tomorrow. And I'll have a check for your shells by then too."

She thanked him, said goodbye, and hurried back to her car. Once she was safely inside she felt tears in her eyes. Relief or pent-up frustration—possibly hope? She couldn't be sure, but she let them flow freely as she drove back to the cottage.

# Seven

ON THANKSGIVING MORNING, Wendy decided the breakfast dishes could wait until later. "We need to go beachcombing," she announced as they put their plates in the sink.

"Can we go right now?" Jackson asked. "The tide's really low—they call it a *minus tide*. And it sounded kinda windy last night. So maybe we'll find something really good out there."

"Let's get our buckets."

Soon they were out on the beach, and after just a few minutes, Jackson gave a happy shriek. He was wearing Poppa's tall rubber boots and was actually wading in the water, claiming that was the best place for good finds. Wendy wasn't so sure, and since she had on tennis shoes, she stayed on the dry side of the surf.

Jackson let out another happy yelp, running toward her. "Mom! *Mom!* I found a sand dollar!"

Wendy hurried closer to see, and sure enough, he had a sand dollar in his hand. Although it was a dull gray color, it was good sized and unbroken. "Jackson!" she exclaimed. "That's fantastic. And it's all in one piece—"

"There's another one!" He bent down to pluck something from the rolling surf.

"You're kidding!" Was it possible he'd actually found two sand dollars? In her whole life she'd never found one.

"It's like I read about online." He held it up. "You gotta go in the water at a minus tide after a storm. Hey, there's another one!" He ran through the water to get it. "I think I hit the mother lode."

Wendy kicked off her shoes, rolled up her jeans, and despite the chilling water, waded in to look as well.

"Another one!" he shrieked.

She ran over to see him putting the fourth sand dollar in his bucket. "That's amazing," she told him.

"I read that people don't find them because they're look-ing for *white* sand dollars, but the sand dollars are mostly gray. Until they're dried out or bleached, they sort of blend with the sand and—hey, there's another." He pointed down through the ankle-deep water. "See it, Mom? It's right there. You can pick it up if you want."

She stared down through the surface of the water, not seeing anything but wet gray sand. And then she noticed a round shape. Bending down, she plucked what was, indeed, a sand dollar. "Wow." She studied it closely. "This is a first for me."

But Jackson was already working his way down the beach and finding more. Perhaps he was right—maybe he had hit the mother lode. She walked a bit farther, staring down at the shallow water, and there, to her shock, she spotted another. "I found another one!" she yelled.

"Great, Mom! Let's keep working this section of beach and see how many we can find before the tide turns."

Wendy continued hunting, letting Jackson direct her toward which section to search. To her amazement she continued to find more sand dollars. Finally, as the bottom of her bucket disappeared, she couldn't help but do a happy dance. "This is so fun!" she cried. "I feel like a pirate discovering a sunken treasure."

"Arrr, matey. We be hauling in the loot," he called back in a good pirate imitation.

Before long, she was as good at spotting the sand dollars as her son, and her bucket was actually getting heavy—making her feel seriously giddy. She couldn't remember when she'd had such a good time—maybe not since childhood. Finally, the tide had fully turned and the water in their "lucky" gathering area grew too deep to continue.

"How many did you get?" she asked Jackson as they stood together at the water's edge.

"I lost count." He held up his bucket to show it was more than half full.

"Me too." She held hers out for him. "Not as much as you though."

He stared out over the rolling waves. "I wish we could get more."

"We'll come again tomorrow," she assured him. "You can check the tide tables and tell me what time we need to be down here."

"All right." He nodded. "Now we gotta take these home and clean 'em."

"How do we clean them?"

"I read how you're supposed to rinse the sand out, then

dip 'em in a bleach solution, rinse 'em again, and let 'em thoroughly dry."

"Well, you're the expert." She ruffled his hair. "Your grandfather would be proud."

Back at the house, they spent about an hour cleaning a grand total of eighty-seven sand dollars. Wendy could hardly believe it as she looked at row after row of gleaming white sand dollars covering every available surface in the kitchen. What would her grandparents say if they could see this?

"Are they valuable, Mom?" He was placing the last ones out to dry on the old towel she'd laid on the kitchen table.

"I honestly don't know. But they're valuable to me."

"I bet we can find even more tomorrow—if we start sooner. You're sure you really wanna go again?"

"You bet I do. I wouldn't miss it. That was so fun."

"But we shouldn't tell anyone about our find." Jackson set the last sand dollar down. "Like when we're having Thanksgiving dinner with those people."

"Why not?" She had already imagined telling Caleb about their amazing luck. She could just imagine how impressed he would be.

"Because we don't want everyone coming out here and looking for our sand dollars."

She laughed. "So we really are pirates, trying to keep our treasure to ourselves? Keeping it a secret?"

"Yeah." He nodded. "Of course!"

Wendy felt nervous as she rang the doorbell. It was the address Caleb had given her, but the house was large and fancy—one of those big beach houses that probably cost a couple million dollars . . . maybe more. Was Caleb really rich? As they waited, she remembered he'd mentioned they'd be eating with his family—and this certainly looked like a family home. Although they'd never discussed their marital status, she'd assumed he was single.

"Is this the right place?" Jackson asked.

"The name Colton was on the mailbox," she explained. "Caleb Colton is who invited us—" She paused as the tall front door opened and a pretty redhead smiled warmly. "You must be Wendy and Jackson. Just the two of you?"

"Yes." Wendy nodded. "That's all."

"I'm Ashley Colton." She shook Wendy's hand and guided them into the foyer. "I'm so glad you could join us. We believe in 'the more the merrier' theory." She took their coats, then led them into a large room where about a dozen other people of varying ages were mingling about. Some appeared to be watching a football game on a big-screen TV while others were just visiting. "Hey, Caleb," Ashley called out. "Why don't you introduce your friends to everyone?"

"Hey, Wendy." Caleb's face broke into a wide smile as he greeted them. "Welcome!" He reached for Jackson's hand, introducing himself.

"I need to get back to the kitchen." Ashley shook her finger at Caleb. "And next time the doorbell rings, you can get it, Mr. Colton."

"Do you need help in the kitchen?" Wendy offered.

"That's okay. I've got Crystal and Beth already helping."

Wendy suspected that was the Crystal from the shell shop—and not eager to cross paths with her again, she just nodded.

"I hope you like to play football," Caleb said to Jackson.

Jackson shrugged. "I used to play soccer."

"He was good too," Wendy told Caleb.

"Great. It's not a real serious game, Jackson, but I need you on my side. Both of you." Caleb lowered his voice. "My cousin Gerard's already bragging he's got this in the bag. I'm pretty sure he's laying bets."

Caleb took them around, introducing them to an aunt and uncle and some cousins, but the names drifted right over her. "And this is Nana," he finally said as they stopped by an elderly woman comfortably seated in a club chair by the fireplace.

"Hello, Wendy and Jackson." The old woman smiled as she grasped Wendy's hand. "I'm pleased to meet you."

"I'm glad to meet you too, uh, Mrs. . . ." Wendy glanced at Caleb. "I didn't catch her last name."

"Just call me *Nana*," the old woman said. "Everyone else does."

"And I'll bet you've met before," Caleb told Nana. "Wendy used to go to your shell shop when she was a girl."

"I thought you looked familiar." Nana nodded knowingly.

"Oh, I doubt you'd possibly remember—"

"You'd be surprised," Caleb told Wendy. "Nana's got a fantastic memory for faces."

Nana peered closely at Wendy. "Did you wear your hair in long pigtails and have freckles on your nose?" she asked. "A summer girl . . . coming here with your grandparents?"

Wendy nodded in amazement. "Yes."

"Your grandparents were the Jacksons . . . and you loved to come in my shop, and you'd look and look at all the shells while your grandparents were in town."

Wendy was shocked. "Yes, you're absolutely right."

Nana's pale blue eyes twinkled. "Then I remember you." She pointed to the ottoman. "Sit down and tell me what you've been doing since then."

Wendy glanced at Jackson, not wanting to leave him out, but to her relief he was engaged with Caleb, telling him about how he'd spent the last few hours laying the checkerboard tiles in the bathroom.

"Did your mom tell you that I helped her pick those tiles out?" Caleb asked.

"No." Jackson shook his head. "But that was a great idea. The floor looks really cool."

"Jackson did a fabulous job," Wendy bragged. "He's quite the handyman."

"But how do you like playing pool?" Caleb asked Jackson. "Or do you prefer Ping-Pong or video games?"

Jackson's eyes lit up. "Yeah, sure—all of the above."

"Great. I've been looking for someone to challenge me. Come on down to the game room and we'll get something going."

With Jackson happily occupied, Wendy wound up giving Caleb's grandma a brief bio of her life, leaving out the sad parts and ending with the inheritance of the cottage.

"Wonderful!" Nana clapped her hands. "Is it just you and your boy in the cottage? Or is there a Mr. Harper around here somewhere?" She glanced over Wendy's shoulder.

Wendy quickly explained about Edward.

"Oh, my. I'm so sorry for your loss." Nana reached for Wendy's hand and gave it a gentle squeeze. "I know that's not easy for a young woman. But I'm so glad you decided to move here. It's such a wonderful place for a boy to grow up."

"Well, we haven't actually moved here . . . not permanently,"

Wendy quietly confessed. "I need to sell the cottage. And go back to my job in Cincinnati."

Nana's brow creased. "Oh, dear, I'm sorry to hear that."

"Unfortunately, my son has assumed we're here for good." Wendy frowned, wishing she hadn't divulged that. Then, in an effort to change the subject, she began telling Nana about finding the sand dollars today. "But please don't tell anyone about it," she said quickly. "I promised Jackson not to tell anyone. It's important to him."

Nana chuckled. "Your secret's safe with me."

"We cleaned them all up and they're drying now," Wendy continued. "I thought maybe I could sell them or something."

"I'm sure you could. Sand dollars are not easily come by 'round here. I'm surprised you found so many . . . although I remember the time my husband and I found about a hundred. All in one day too. Lewis was just home from the war and we were newly married. Living in a fisherman's shack. But with all those sand dollars, we thought we were rich." She laughed heartily. "As it turned out, we were."

"When did you first start your shell shop?"

"It was the summer of 1946. Not long after we found all those sand dollars. Lewis was working as a fisherman. We used his GI loan to buy the property in town, and we moved into the apartment up above. He continued to fish, and I started up the shop. When I wasn't working at the shop, I was out on the beach hunting for shells. That's how I got most of my original inventory—out there on the beach."

"What a lovely way to live."

She sighed. "It was . . . oh, it really was."

Wendy didn't know what to say now. Nana appeared far away, and she hated to disturb her.

"Not everyone would agree with me about this"—Nana lowered her voice—"but I truly believe that people are happier with less . . . not more." She glanced around the spacious room with its high ceilings, expensive furnishings, and enormous fireplace. "This house is far too much for my taste."

"I was pretty surprised Caleb has such a fancy house," Wendy admitted.

"Oh, no, this isn't Caleb's house," Nana corrected. "This is his parents' home. They're down in Palm Beach for the winter. They just let the kids use this place for get-togethers. Ashley is in charge."

"Is Ashley Caleb's wife?" Wendy asked quietly, almost wishing she hadn't.

"Oh, goodness, no." Nana shook her head. "Ashley is Caleb's baby sister."

"Oh." Wendy wondered if Nana could see through her question.

"Caleb isn't married. In fact, he's gotten a reputation for being a confirmed bachelor." She chuckled. "But I never give up hope."

Before Wendy could respond, Ashley began calling everyone into an elegant dining room, where it didn't take long for all eighteen of the guests to take their places around an enormous table that looked out over the ocean. Caleb sat at one end of the table with Nana on the other end. He led them in a blessing then asked everyone to share one thing they were thankful for.

"I'm thankful for my family and friends," he began. "And for new friends too."

Wendy felt nervous as they went around the table, unsure of what she'd say—especially since she hadn't been particularly thankful for anything lately. Well, besides the sand dollars, and she'd been sworn to secrecy about that. Finally, it was her turn, and there was only one honest answer. "I'm thankful for my son, Jackson," she said. "He's been so helpful in coming back to Seaside. I couldn't possibly do this without him."

When Jackson's turn came, she braced herself. "I'm thankful that I get to live in Seaside—the most beautiful place in the world!"

Everyone cheered, but Wendy felt like crawling under the table. How long could she let him go on living in a delusion? As they started to pass food around, she felt Nana's eyes upon her. But the wise old woman simply smiled in a knowing way—almost as if she understood.

To Wendy's relief, Jackson appeared perfectly relaxed and at ease with everyone, comfortably making conversations with those around him. Wendy tried to calm her nerves and follow his example, even making small talk with Crystal, who was seated next to her. But she couldn't help but think this all felt strangely surreal—like she was someone else or playing a role in a movie. And yet, she realized it was surprisingly enjoyable too. For the most part, Caleb's friends and family were disarmingly likable. Well, except for Crystal. Wendy still didn't know what to make of her. The way the pretty blonde shared details about Caleb's life, his likes and dislikes and personal history, well, it became clear that this woman had territorial feelings toward Caleb. For all Wendy knew, they were practically engaged. Or at least Crystal acted like it.

Still, the rest of them were great, and by the time they went outside to play football, Wendy almost felt like one of the family. Glad that she'd worn jeans, Wendy sat on a log to remove her suede boots and put on tennis shoes, listening as Caleb and Gerard bantered over who was on which team.

"Wendy and Jackson are my guests, so they're on my team," Caleb declared.

"Then I get Rick and Curtis," Gerard told him.

"Don't forget me," Crystal cooed and, stepping next to Caleb, linked her arm in his. "Remember how I helped you win last year?"

Before long they were playing, running the football up and down the beach. And although Caleb kept assuring Wendy it was just a "friendly game," she couldn't help but notice how badly Gerard wanted to win. He tossed out good-natured jabs and took advantage of the situation whenever he could.

Caleb, on the other hand, was more laid-back, doing an admirable job of encouraging his teammates. He also gave Jackson lots of opportunities to handle the ball. Because of Caleb's good attitude, Wendy was determined to put forth a good effort. He didn't know that she'd grown up playing sports and could still run pretty fast. But Crystal seemed intent on monopolizing most of the plays, insisting that she had it under control. Unfortunately, Crystal could neither catch nor run—and their team was falling steadily behind.

"I'll receive the next pass," Wendy finally told Caleb as their team huddled together.

"Really?" He looked surprised. "You want to?"

"Let her," Jackson urged. "She's really fast—I mean, for a mom anyway."

Caleb's eyes lit up. "Okay then." He told her a plan and where to run, and when the time came, she did exactly as told and they easily scored.

"Woo-hoo!" Caleb hooted as he gave her a high-five. "Our secret weapon has finally arrived."

It wasn't long until their team caught up. Just seconds before Nana sounded the blow-horn—according to the kitchen timer in her lap—Jackson caught a sloppy bilateral pass from Wendy and scored the winning touchdown. Caleb grabbed up Jackson and Wendy, giving them a bear hug before they were mobbed by the rest of their teammates in a victory celebration. Everyone except Crystal. She was standing on the sidelines, inspecting a broken fingernail with a furrowed brow. Wendy attempted a smile as she and Jackson passed by, but Crystal just glowered.

After football, it was time for dessert, followed by some rowdy charades. But when it started getting dusky out, and Wendy couldn't help but notice the chill coming from Crystal's direction, she felt it was time to go. No need to overstay their welcome. She thanked everyone and said a personal goodbye to Nana. Then Caleb walked her and Jackson out to the car. Before she got in, he handed her a couple of magazines.

"Just some old catalogues," he explained. "In case you decide to make some beachy accessories from your shell collection. These are from last year, but the ideas are still good. And you can see, these items, when done right, can go for some pretty high prices. Not a bad way to make a living if you're so inclined."

"Thanks, I can't wait to go through them."

He slapped his forehead. "And I just remembered—I totally forgot your payment for the shells. I made you a check and left it in my woodshop." He smiled. "Maybe you could drop by and pick it up."

"Sure." She nodded. "That's fine. Will your store be open?"

"Yes. As part of the SDA, I don't have a choice these next few days."

"SDA?"

"Seaside Downtown Association."

"They force you to be open?"

"Well, we all agreed to be open. You see, this weekend is Small Business Saturday. Everyone is supposed to be open. The hope is that there'll be lots of Christmas shoppers. And then there's the tree lighting in the town square—and all the businesses' Christmas lights will come on too. That happens on Saturday evening at five." He tipped his head toward Jackson. "Remind your mom to bring you. It's pretty fun. We all sing carols and drink cocoa and eat cookies."

"Sounds cool," Jackson told him.

"Hey, how are you at hanging Christmas lights?" Caleb asked Jackson.

Jackson shrugged. "I don't really know."

"You mind being on a ladder?"

Jackson grinned. "Not at all."

"Because I could use a hand. I still haven't put my lights up. You interested in a paying job?"

Jackson's eyes lit up. "Yeah, sure. That'd be great. When?"

"Well, as the town's worst procrastinator, I don't usually put my lights up until just moments before the town lighting. Drives my sister nuts." He rubbed his chin. "How about three o'clock on Saturday. It shouldn't take us much more than an hour to get 'er done."

"Is that okay?" Jackson asked Wendy.

"That's fine," she told him. With that settled, they told Caleb goodbye and headed for home. As Wendy drove, she felt tired, but it was a happy sort of exhaustion. Better than she'd felt in a long time. Despite the fact that their cottage was in total disrepair and they still didn't have a real bathroom, she felt glad to be going home. "Today was a good day," she told Jackson as she drove down the beach road.

"It totally was," Jackson declared. "And Thanksgiving was way better than I thought it would be. I actually like your friends, Mom. And Caleb is pretty cool."

"They're not exactly *my* friends," she confessed. "I mean, other than Caleb, and I barely know him. But, really, you know all of them just as well as I do."

"Well, they were pretty cool. Even Gerard was okay. He got a little intense, but he was nice about congratulating us when we finally won."

"I think he was surprised."

"But I'm not sure about that Crystal chick."

"Oh?"

"No offense, but she didn't seem to like you, Mom."

Wendy told him about the incident at the shell shop. "We didn't exactly get off on the right foot."

"I think she's jealous."

"Jealous?"

"Yeah. Because Caleb likes you better than he likes her."

"Oh, I don't know about—"

"It was obvious, Mom. Couldn't you see it?"

"I'm not sure." To change the subject, she told him about Caleb's grandmother, and how amazing it was that she remembered Wendy from so many years ago. "Nana is such a darling old lady—and I hope you don't mind but I told her about our sand dollars."

"Mom!"

"She promised not to breathe a word of it." Now she told him about how Nana found sand dollars so long ago. "They got a hundred in one day, Jackson. And that was partly why she started the shell shop. I know we can trust her not to tell anyone. And she loved hearing about it."

"Okay then . . . You didn't tell anyone else? Not even Caleb?"

"No—I didn't tell anyone else."

"And we're still going out tomorrow morning? First thing?"

"You bet we are." As she pulled into the driveway, the wheels in her head were already spinning—imagining ways she might be able to use their sand dollars as well as the other multitudes of shells her grandparents had found to make objects that could be sold. She knew they wouldn't get rich from selling shell art, but if she could just help cover some of their expenses before her credit card went up in a puff of smoke, she would be most grateful.

# Eight

AS THEY STARTED up to the front porch, Wendy heard a scuffling sound. Grabbing Jackson's hand, she began to back up, digging in her jacket pocket for her phone. It was too dusky to see well, and they hadn't left any lights on. With a trembling hand, Wendy prepared to call 911. It figured that after such a perfect day, they'd come home to a burglar!

"What is it?" Jackson whispered as she tugged him toward the car.

"Someone on the porch," she hissed. "Get in the car and—"

"Look, Mom!" He pointed toward the porch. "It's just a dog."

"What?" She lowered her phone, peering through the darkness.

"It's a dog." Jackson let go of her hand and hurried toward the house. "Hey, dog," he said gently. "What're you doing here?"

Sure enough, an energetic dog bounded down the steps, wagging its tail as Jackson knelt to greet it. "It's friendly,"

Jackson said as she rushed over. She unlocked the front door and turned on the porch light, revealing a midsized dog. It appeared to be a mixed breed—maybe some terrier as well as some shepherd, but the dog's expression and wagging tail suggested friendliness.

"Where did you come from?" Wendy knelt to see that the dog's shaggy coat was matted and dirty. "Any ID?"

"He doesn't have a collar," Jackson told her.

"How do you know it's a he?" she asked.

Jackson snickered. "Some things are obvious, Mom."

"Oh, well." She stood up. "What do we do with him?"

"I think we should feed him," Jackson told her. "I can feel his ribs."

"Oh, I don't know." She wasn't sure about taking a stray dog into the house. "Maybe we should call someone . . . to get him."

"It's Thanksgiving, Mom. Who are you gonna call?"

Wendy shrugged. "Good point."

"Are you hungry, boy?" Jackson opened the door. "Wanna come in and have some food?"

Without hesitating, the dog followed Jackson inside, while Wendy turned on more lights. The cottage was just as messy as they'd left it. She remembered her fear over a possible burglar, but decided a smart thief would probably take one look at this place and run the other way. She went into the kitchen where their sand dollars were still spread all over the place. "What should we feed him?" She opened the fridge and looked.

"How about eggs?" Jackson suggested.

"Eggs?" She frowned.

"Yeah, they're protein. And if he hasn't eaten for a while, they might go down easily."

She couldn't help but smile. "Since when did you get to be such an expert on dogs?"

He shrugged as he removed the egg carton. "I'll fix his food for him, Mom. You don't have to do a thing."

"Okay." She stepped back, frowning down at the dog. "He's really dirty, Jackson. And for all we know he could have fleas or mange or, well, anything. After you feed him, you better put him back outside for the night."

"Aw, Mom."

"Jackson." She put a warning in her tone.

"But he needs a friend right now," Jackson pleaded. "What if I clean him up?"

"We don't even have a working bathroom," she pointed out.

"The shower works okay," he reminded her.

She rolled her eyes. "Fine, clean him up if you want."

"Thanks, Mom."

"And don't make a mess in the bathroom."

"Don't worry. I won't."

"You'll have to take complete responsibility for the dog tonight, and tomorrow morning we'll try to figure out who he belongs to . . . or take him to a shelter or something. Okay?"

He reluctantly agreed. Feeling like she might be making a mistake, she went into the living room and let out a long sigh. She'd already started dismantling this room and even painted two walls. But right now it looked disheveled and overwhelming. Besides the rest of the painting, which she planned to attack tomorrow, the wood floors really needed some attention. And she needed to thin out a lot more, including clearing some of the old, bulky pieces of furniture. Somehow she should stage this room, and with no budget to buy anything extra, she'd have to rely on her ingenuity and elbow grease.

But the living room could wait. Right now she needed to focus on her bedroom. After getting the walls painted yesterday, she'd spent several hours scrubbing the soft pine floor earlier today. To her relief, it was dry and looked pretty good. Now she just needed to paint the baseboard and window trim with the white paint. Later she'd get Jackson to help her move the furniture back into place—and call it a night.

Scooting along the floor, she carefully painted the wood trim. She could hear Christmas music drifting in from the living room and knew Jackson must've put an old record on. The cheery music combined with Jackson thumping around and happily chattering at the dog filled the little cottage with a sweet, homey sound. Almost like a real family.

She was just putting the lid back on the paint can when Jackson knocked on her door. "Wanna see Oliver, Mom?"

"Oliver?" She cautiously opened the door to see that not only did the dog appear clean and groomed, he had what appeared to be a leather collar around his neck. "Wow." She knelt down to examine him better and noticed he even smelled good. "How did you—"

"I kinda had to shower with him." Jackson grinned, and she noticed that his hair was still damp and he'd changed into sweats. "Then I went through that storage room upstairs. Remember I put some of your stuff up there too—and there was an old hairbrush and comb set that I used to comb out his hair. I had to cut some of the mats out."

"Where did you get *this*?" She fingered the soft leather collar.

"It was an old belt that was in a pile of men's clothes, but it was all worn out where the holes used to be, so I cut it down and made a new hole. I hope you don't mind."

"It was probably Poppa's." She smiled wistfully. "You're a clever young man, Jackson."

"He's a really good dog, Mom. He didn't even mind when I used the hairdryer on him."

"My hairdryer?"

"Yeah, but I took good care of it and put it back in your stuff."

She stood up and, folding her arms across her front, tried to think of a gentle way to put the kibosh on this dog business.

"And he's real smart, Mom. Oliver already knows how to sit and stay."

"Oliver?"

"That just seemed like his name."

"Really?"

Jackson glanced past her. "Hey, Mom, this room looks really great. That color you mixed up is really cool. Can I paint my room a color too?"

"What color would you choose?"

"How about a darker blue? Maybe like the ocean on a cloudy day."

She slowly nodded. "I suppose that'd be okay. We just need to be sure we select colors that buyers like."

Jackson got that stubborn look again, but then he smiled. "Everyone likes blue, Mom."

She pointed to Oliver. "And don't forget that he is only here for the night." Jackson's smile vanished and Wendy felt like a villain. "How about if you help me get the furniture pieces back in here?" she asked.

"Okay," he muttered.

"We need to be careful not to bump the wood I just painted—it's still tacky." She looked at the dog. "Will he be okay?"

"I'll put him in my room," Jackson said glumly. "I fixed him up a bed and water bowl and everything up there. He really likes it too."

It didn't take long to get the few furnishings into place, but when they were finished, Jackson still looked like he'd lost his best friend—or was about to. Wendy felt guilty and knew somehow she needed to put a better spin on this.

"Here's the deal," she began carefully. "You said yourself that the dog seems well trained . . . and that probably means he has an owner—*somewhere*. I'm guessing he could belong to a tourist. Maybe he got lost on the beach. If we get the word out, someone will probably claim him. He might even have an electronic chip to identify him. A lot of people get those for pets. He does seem like a nice dog—"

"So you *do* like him?"

She smiled. "Of course. What's not to like? But he probably has a heartbroken owner who loves and misses him. And here's the bottom line, Jackson—I just don't want you to be too hurt when that happens."

"But what if no one shows up to claim him?" Jackson asked with hopeful eyes. "Could I keep him then?"

Wendy didn't know what to say. Their apartment back in Cincinnati had a strict no-pets policy, but she wasn't ready to have that conversation. Not tonight. "Oh, Jackson." She sighed, pushing hair away from her face. "I don't know. Let's just sleep on it. Okay?"

"Okay." He nodded. "That's fair."

"And tomorrow, you can ask around the neighborhood—see if anyone knows who he belongs to."

"All right, Mom. I'll do that." Jackson wrapped his arms around her neck, solidly kissing her cheek. "Good night, Mom."

"Good night." She ruffled his hair.

"And I'll sleep tight," he added. "I'll sleep even better than usual because I've got a watchdog in my room."

Wendy resisted the urge to groan as she forced a smile, then closed her door. She knew she was in over her head—more with each passing day. Somehow, she had to get through this without losing her son . . . or her mind. Remembering her promise to Jackson—to trust God more—she decided to pray about this latest addition to their household. "Dear God," she pleaded quietly and quickly, "please help us to find that lost dog's real owners. Amen."

Wendy was pleasantly surprised to wake to sunshine streaming through the bare window the next morning. She'd removed the tattered curtain before painting the bedroom, and although she had some ideas for recycling linens, she hadn't figured out the new window covering yet. At least she'd taken the time to clean the glass, and with the morning sunshine, it was sparkling.

"Good morning," Jackson called out as she came into the kitchen. "Oliver and I already went down to the beach." He held up a bucket. "I found about thirty sand dollars."

"I totally forgot," Wendy admitted. "You should've woken me."

"I figured you needed to sleep in, Mom. You've been working so hard lately."

"Thanks. That was nice." Wendy filled the coffeepot with water.

"I met one of our neighbors on the beach. A girl about my age. She and her mom and little sister are renting a cottage about ten houses down the beach from us. She said it looks just like ours except that it's yellow."

"And she lives here full-time? Or are they just here for the weekend?" She measured coffee grounds into the basket.

"They're full-timers. She said they moved here last summer after her parents got divorced. Her mom works as a waitress at Fisherman's Wharf."

"Wow, you learned a lot about her."

"She's a real talker." Jackson grinned. "I guess she was nice to me because I gave her some sand dollars."

Wendy felt her brows arch as she turned on the coffee maker. "You gave up some of your precious sand dollars?"

"Well, the tide was already in and she couldn't believe how many I'd found. And she's never found any before. I guess I felt sorry for her."

"Uh-huh." Wendy noticed the empty egg carton in the trash and the frying pan still on the stove. "Did you finish off the eggs?" she asked.

"Me and Oliver." He grinned sheepishly. "I put some cheese in them too."

"Sounds delish." She put a slice of bread in the toaster.

"Anyway, Taylor told me she's seen Oliver out on the beach before, but that he'd never come to her when she called for him. She figured he must really like me a lot."

"So does, uh, Taylor know where Oliver might live? Or who might own him?"

"Nope, but she offered to help me ask around. I guess she knows almost everyone who lives along here."

"Taylor sounds like a very friendly girl."

"Yeah, she is." He pointed out the window. "There she is now. She had to go home for a little bit, but said she'd be back to walk around with me—you know, to look for Oliver's owners . . . like I promised you I'd do."

"Good for her."

Jackson opened the back door, calling out to a spindly girl with wild red curls that bounced as she ran. Jackson greeted her and even invited her into the house and then, acting like a perfect gentleman, introduced her to Wendy.

"I've been hearing about you," Wendy told her. "That's nice of you to help Jackson find Oliver's owners. I'm sure that some family is missing him."

"I doubt it," Taylor said in a matter-of-fact tone. "I think Oliver is an abandoned stray or runaway. He probably got left behind by one of those summer families. Maybe they were mean to him or they just didn't want him anymore or couldn't afford his dog food."

"Oh?" Wendy didn't know how to respond.

"But Jackson is a good master for Oliver. They get along real nice. I tried to make friends with Oliver before—well, I didn't call him Oliver *then* since I didn't know his name, but I do think Oliver fits him. Don't you?"

"It's a nice name."

"Anyway, even when I took a hot dog out on the beach, that dog wouldn't give me the time of day. That's probably good since my mom won't let me have a dog anyway." She poked Jackson. "We better get moving, man. I have to be home by eleven so Mom can get to work on time." She turned back to Wendy with a wrinkled nose. "I have to babysit my little sister." She rolled her eyes. "Tessa is only six, but she can be a royal pain in the you-know-what. But at least Mom pays me for babysitting. Well, if her tips are good enough."

"Come on, Oliver." Jackson tied what looked like a piece of clothesline onto the leather collar. "Let's go and see if we can find your *owners*." He made a snickering sound that suggested this was a pointless mission, but that he was willing to jump through these silly hoops—just to placate his mom.

Wendy watched as Jackson, his loquacious new friend, and the devoted dog headed down the beach road together. She hadn't seen that much spring in her son's step for a long time . . . and the prospect of taking it from him made her feel sick inside. What had she gotten herself into—and how on earth would she ever get out?

# Nine

WHILE GORDON REINSTALLED the bathroom fixtures, Wendy perused the cluttered storage room in search of items she could recycle or up-cycle in staging the cottage. Her plan was to create a sort of shabby-chic décor. Not too cluttered or overly sweet, but just charming and beachy and inviting. Hopefully it would entice a buyer to pay top dollar—ASAP.

The more she poked and dug, exploring the tiny attic space and jam-packed linen closet, the more she realized she was on a real treasure hunt. Everyday items left behind by her grandparents and other ancestors who'd inhabited this cottage suddenly took on new meaning. By the time Jackson came home, she'd sorted her finds into several piles. One stack was old linens and textiles that she planned to recycle into lace trimmed curtains, quaint pillow covers, and table-cloths. She'd even dug out a nicely worn patchwork quilt. Its faded pastel shades, combined with the enamel white headboard she'd unearthed in the attic, would look lovely in her pale blue bedroom.

She'd also found old lamps, picture frames, mirrors, boxes,

and vases that she hoped to reinvent into one-of-a-kind home accessories that could be sold in town or even used to stage the cottage. After perusing the catalogues Caleb had given her, she was full of ideas for using driftwood, shells, and sea glass . . . for profit. Caleb hadn't exaggerated about the price tags on artisan-made beach décor. If she only created and sold a few pieces, it would help cover some expenses.

But her favorite find in her morning explorations was an old wooden box tucked way back in the tiny attic space. Besides a dozen vintage paint-by-number seascapes that she wanted to frame with driftwood, the box also contained old family photos dating clear back to the late 1800s. She picked up a sepia-toned photograph of a young couple, studying it, curious to see if there was any family resemblance.

"Who's that?" Jackson peered over her shoulder to see.

"These are your great-great-grandparents." She flipped the photo over to show him where Poppa had written "My parents, Odell and Viola Jackson, 1909."

"That's more than a hundred years ago." Jackson took the picture, examining it more closely.

"I think they were the original owners of this cottage."

"Wow, that is so cool, Mom. We should hang their picture in our house." He reached into the box for another old photo. "We should hang all these up. It could be our way to remember the past, kind of like saying thank you to them for giving us this cool place to live." He looked hopefully at her. "Wouldn't they look great on the fireplace mantel? Or we could just hang them on the wall. How about along the stairway? I've seen that before in movies."

"I don't know . . ." She wanted to say "no way," because she knew family photos weren't the best way to stage a house.

And yet it was sweet that he appreciated his family history. "Do you really want all these old ancestors staring down on you? Isn't it kind of creepy?"

"They're our family, Mom. It would be like they're here with us, watching over us."

"Well, I'll think about it." She slowly stood. "What about Oliver? Any luck finding his owner?"

"Nah. Mrs. Campbell agrees with Taylor. She thinks one of the summer families abandoned him a couple months ago. She told me I should just keep him. And that reminds me, we should go get him some dog food today. And we probably need some other groceries too. We're out of eggs, and I just finished the last of the milk."

"Hallo up there," Gordon called from downstairs. "I'm all finished in the bathroom. Wanna come have a look?"

As they clomped down the stairs to check out his work, Wendy knew this meant she'd have to give Gordon his final payment, and her resources were pretty tapped out. Still, having the bathroom done put them that much closer to selling. Somehow she had to stretch her budget to make these frazzled ends meet.

"I missed having my good work assistant with me today," Gordon told Jackson.

"I'm sorry." Jackson introduced him to Oliver, explaining his hunt for the dog's owners.

"Looks like a good dog." Gordon gently twisted Oliver's ear. "Maybe you oughta keep 'im. Make a good watchdog."

"Yeah, that's what I told Mom."

"It's possible he belongs to someone else," Wendy said a bit sharply.

"Take him down to the vet clinic," Gordon told her. "They

get lost dogs in there all the time. They got a bulletin board for it too."

"Wow, this looks like a *real* bathroom." Jackson was already in the bathroom, probably trying to segue their conversation. "You even put up the towel bars and stuff. It looks really good."

Wendy hurried past Gordon to see for herself. "It's perfect!" she said. "Thank you so much! It really does look like a bathroom now. Better than ever."

"Well, you and your boy did the flooring and paint—and if you ask me, it's not half bad either." He handed her his bill.

She knew Gordon didn't take credit cards, but even if he did, she wasn't sure there was enough left on her card to cover this. "I'll get my checkbook," she told him. As she went to her bedroom, she felt a desperate rush of nerves. Her anemic checking account didn't have quite enough to cover this, but she hated to ask Gordon to wait. She remembered the seashells that Caleb had made a check for. If she could pick that up and deposit it today, it would probably make up the difference. At least she hoped so. Just to be safe, she dated the check for tomorrow, and fortunately, when she explained it to Gordon, he didn't seem to mind.

"Probably won't make it to the bank until Monday anyway." He slipped it into his pocket. "Feel free to call me if you need help with anything else."

She thanked him, and as soon as he left, she told Jackson they needed to run to town. She pointed to Oliver. "But what do we do with him?"

"Can't he come with us?"

She considered this. "Good idea. I think I'll take Gordon's advice and swing by the vet clinic to—"

"Do I have to go with you to town?" Jackson said. "If I stay home, I can start clearing out my room, you know, get it ready to paint."

"That's true."

"Maybe you could bring home some dark blue paint."

"I suppose I could." If Caleb's check was big enough to cover it.

"And Oliver can keep me company. Like Gordon said, he's a good watchdog. He really makes me feel safe, Mom. You know, when I'm home alone . . . or walking on the beach."

Wendy could tell she was being manipulated, but it was hard to argue. Besides, it would be easier to run errands—and go to the vet clinic—without Jackson and Oliver tagging along. "Okay," she agreed. "But you both stay in the house while I'm gone. If you need anything, call me. I should be back in an hour."

As she parked in front of the hardware store, Wendy thought of a few more items that she could use from there . . . except she didn't have the funds. However, she remembered how Poppa had kept an account with the store. She wondered if they still did that, or if she could open one. By the time they sent her first bill, she'd have sold the cottage and could easily repay them with interest if necessary.

But first things first. She needed to get and deposit that check. Like he'd promised, Caleb's store was open but, to her dismay, Crystal was working there today. "I, uh, I thought you worked next door," Wendy said tentatively.

"I work here . . . and there . . . wherever they need me," Crystal said lightly. "It's all in the family." She laughed. "So are you furniture shopping?"

"No, I'm here to see Caleb." Wendy forced what she hoped looked like a friendly smile.

"Caleb's busy." Crystal smiled but her eyes seemed chilly. "He's got this big dining table project to complete. It's this amazing piece of live-edge wood and two benches and several chairs. Really beautiful. Anyway, he's got to get it finished by early next week. He does *not* want to be disturbed."

"Oh." Wendy pursed her lips.

"Sorry." Crystal looked a bit smug.

Wendy remained at the counter, trying to think of something. "Well, Caleb asked me to come by," she told Crystal. "He had something for me." She looked around. "Or maybe he left it out here."

Crystal frowned. "I have absolutely no idea what you're talking about."

"It's just that he told me he'd be here and to come—"

"Fine." Crystal's tone grew sharp. "I'll go check with him. But I do hate to interrupt his work. Caleb is an artist, you know. He really shouldn't be disturbed."

"I'm sorry, it's just that—"

"Never mind, I'm going." And just like that she disappeared into the back room.

Wendy felt guilty as she waited. Maybe it really was wrong to disturb him like this. But, really, wouldn't it only take a minute or two? When Crystal didn't come right back, Wendy felt even more guilty.

"Hello?" a female voice called from the front of the store. "Anyone here?"

"I'm here." Wendy went over to see an older couple standing by a coffee table.

"Oh, good." The woman pointed to the table. "What can you tell us about that?"

"Well, it's handmade by a very talented local artist whose work sells all around the country." Wendy smiled nervously. "Caleb Colton is the craftsman. He makes all the wood furnishings in this shop. Each is a one-of-a-kind piece. Completely unique." She glanced at the tag on the table, trying not to blink at the price. "And as you can see, this one is made from black walnut. Caleb uses all sorts of wood." She reached down to stroke the smooth surface. "Isn't this wood grain amazing?"

"Yes." The woman nodded. "I absolutely love it—and it would look perfect in our great room."

"It's rustic yet elegant." Wendy wished she could afford such a piece for the cottage.

"Well, then I guess we better get it," the man said. "I assume you deliver?"

"I, uh, yes, of course," Wendy assured him. If Caleb didn't deliver, Wendy felt certain it would fit in the back of her Subaru. And for the price of this piece, Caleb would be a fool not to provide free delivery.

"Then write it up," the man instructed.

Wendy was just going up to the counter when Caleb emerged. Wearing work clothes, a fine coating of sawdust, and a warm smile, he greeted her.

"I just sold your walnut coffee table," she whispered to him. "What?"

"That couple over there—they assumed I worked here and I just played along. Do you deliver?"

"You bet." He chuckled. "Nice work, Wendy."

"You folks are in luck," Wendy told the couple. "You'll

get to meet the artist now." And just like that she introduced Caleb to them—and they all visited congenially, discussing the walnut table and where Caleb found the wood for it.

"We just closed on a beach house a few miles out of town," the man explained. "We hope to be in by Christmas—and she hopes to have it all furnished by then." He shook his head at his wife like this was doubtful.

"I don't expect it to be completely furnished," his wife told him. "But I would like it to be comfortable for when the family comes." She turned to Wendy. "I just haven't been able to find the perfect dining table yet."

"Caleb is working on a beautiful dining table right now," Wendy told them. Okay, she could barely remember seeing it the other day when she'd been in his woodshop, but she had no doubt it would be beautiful. "But I do believe it's a commissioned piece. Right, Caleb?"

"Yes, it's a whole dining set that I hope to finish in the next few days."

"How long does it take to make a dining table?" the woman asked.

"Depends." He rubbed his chin. "On my schedule . . . and what sort of table you're wanting . . . and whether I have the right products on hand." As the woman described what she hoped to find, Caleb flipped through a notebook of photos, showing her various tables he'd made in the past.

"This is it!" The woman pointed to a live-edge maple table with black metal legs. "I need it long enough to seat ten people. Can you do that?"

Caleb nodded. "Let me look into my wood supply and get back to you on it." They were just exchanging business cards when Crystal returned to the shop. Wendy couldn't help but wonder what she'd been doing all this time, but had no intention of asking.

"Crystal will write up today's purchase for you," Caleb told the couple. "And she'll arrange for delivery." He shook their hands. "And hopefully we'll come up with a plan to get you folks a dining table in time for Christmas."

As they thanked him, Caleb led Wendy to the back room, and after closing the door behind him, he picked up an envelope with her name on it. "Is this what you came for?"

"Yes, but I feel bad for interrupting your work," she said quickly. "I know your time is precious and you need to get this finished." She ran her hand over the smooth tabletop. "It's beautiful."

"Uh-huh." Suddenly he tore the envelope into pieces and dropped it into a trash can of shavings.

"Oh." Wendy didn't know what to say. "I hope I didn't overstep my bounds just now . . . I didn't know what—"

Caleb just laughed as he pulled open a drawer and, removing a checkbook, started to write. "Sorry, I didn't mean to alarm you. But my salespeople work on commission. And that means I owe you for the walnut table and—"

"Oh, no, you don't have to—"

"I probably should include you on the commissioned table too. After all, you were the one to mention that to her." His blue eyes twinkled. "Nicely done."

"But I didn't expect to—"

"It's only fair." He tore off the check. "I just thought it'd be easier to simply write one check—with both the shells and commission. Here you go."

"Well, thank you." She had to stop herself from spilling

the truth—just how badly she needed this right now. "I appreciate it."

"I appreciate your salesmanship." He grinned. "Maybe you'll consider working here . . . well, once the season really starts in the late spring. In the meantime, I've got an agreement with my sister and mom to share employees during the off-season. Crystal kind of floats between shops." He grimaced.

"That makes sense. And now I'll let you get back to your work. I know you don't want any distractions."

"Hey, some distractions are most welcome." His smile sent a happy rush through her.

"Well, I, uh, I left Jackson home alone." She felt her face growing warm as she explained about Oliver. "And I need to get dog food and more paint and some other things—and I have to be home in an hour and . . . well, I better go." She knew she sounded foolish, but couldn't help herself.

"And how about tomorrow?" Caleb picked up a wood plane, blowing a curly shaving out of it. "Jackson still planning to help me hang lights at three?"

She nodded. "He's counting on it."

Caleb grinned. "See you then."

As she went back into the store, Wendy suppressed the urge to giggle like a schoolgirl, but when she saw Crystal's icy glare, her giddiness evaporated.

"Did you know that those people actually assumed you worked here?" Crystal demanded. "Were you trying to pass yourself off as—"

"I wasn't trying to pass as anything," Wendy responded firmly. "I only wanted to help—to make sure Caleb didn't lose a customer."

"Caleb's customers are *my* responsibility. You could've gotten me."

"I'm sorry. I didn't want to disturb Caleb, and I thought you'd be right back."

"I suppose I should *thank you* for your help." Crystal's tone sounded sarcastic. "But in the future, I'd prefer to handle *our* customers myself."

Wendy suddenly remembered the commission Caleb had added to her check. How would Crystal react to that? Hopefully Wendy would never have to find out. "Sorry to interfere." Wendy moved toward the door. "See you around."

As she hurried out, Wendy felt like she'd poked a hornets' nest. For whatever reason, and there were probably plenty, Crystal appeared to have targeted Wendy. And like Jackson had pointed out after Thanksgiving, Crystal made no secret of her interest in Caleb. Although Wendy felt fairly certain that Caleb's interest in Crystal was minimal, Crystal was clearly marking her territory wherever Caleb was concerned. And that was fine. Because really, why would Wendy want to upset anything? She and Jackson would be long gone in a few weeks—maybe sooner if all went well. Wendy's best hope of getting out of debt and putting their lives back on track hadn't changed. She needed to sell that cottage, hopefully soon, and go back to her job in Cincinnati.

# Ten

WENDY FELT a sense of accomplishment as she carried her packages into the cottage. Her trip to town had paid off nicely. Not only had she deposited money to cover Gordon's check, she had enough remaining to buy groceries, get gas, and have a little cash left over. She opened a credit account at the hardware store and got Jackson's paint and a number of other things necessary for getting the cottage into tip-top shape. Finally, she stopped by the veterinarian clinic to check the "lost pets" bulletin board. Unfortunately, no one had reported a missing dog that sounded anything like Oliver. Just the same, she'd filled out a "found dog" card and prominently posted it. It wasn't as eye-catching as the ones with photos, but it was better than nothing. Hopefully someone would claim Oliver before it was time to return to Ohio.

"I got your paint," she called up the stairway.

"Great," Jackson bounded down the stairs with Oliver behind him. "I got my room all cleared out and just finished masking off the baseboard and window like you told me to do."

She handed him the can. "It's called Sailor's Sea Blue."

"Cool name! I wanna get started right now."

"I need your help first." She explained that her goal was to get the kitchen cabinets painted today. "But before I begin, I want to peel the old floor covering up. Otherwise it could mess up the freshly painted cabinets. Anyway, I could use some help."

"Yeah, I was wondering about that floor. It's pretty creepy."

"Hopefully it'll come up easily. It's been there for as long as I can remember."

Jackson started to tug on a curling corner. "There's not much holding it down."

"I thought we might put down more checkerboard floor like in the bathroom." She jerked up a large piece, pulling it back to reveal wide planks of wood. "But, hey, this is nice." She touched the pale grain. "I think it's pine."

"Can we just use it as our kitchen floor?"

"I don't see why not." Before long, they had all the old ugly vinyl removed and piled in the junk pile that Gordon had promised to remove on Monday. Back in the kitchen they both admired the rustic yet handsome wood floor. "We can probably sand down these old patches of glue." Wendy swept the debris into the dustpan.

"I think it's lots nicer than that other floor. I wonder why they ever covered it up."

"They probably thought the vinyl was more modern." She dumped the dustpan. "But I love this."

"So can I go paint my room now?" he asked. "I really want to see what color it's going to be."

"Let's keep Oliver down here while you're painting." She patted the dog's head. "I got him some dog food." She reached into a bag from the hardware store. "And this." She produced a sturdy red leash.

"Thanks, Mom!" He hugged her then turned to the dog. "Okay, Oliver." He pointed a finger. "You stay here with Mom until I get finished and then, if there's time, I'll take you down to the beach."

Oliver wagged his tail like he understood as Wendy dug out a chipped mixing bowl and filled it with dry dog food. She carried this and his water bowl out to the laundry room. "You stay here for a while," she told him. "I've got some painting to do."

As Wendy opened the can of turquoise paint, she hoped it wasn't too bold. A potential buyer could be turned off by a strong choice. Even so, she liked it. She'd already masked off the glass panes in the upper cabinets and spread out the plastic drop cloths that Caleb had encouraged her to buy to protect the countertops and wood floors. Feeling a bit nervous over this color choice, she started to paint.

By that evening, she had all the upper cabinets painted. She stepped back to survey her work. Was it too much? She wasn't sure, but the turquoise color simply made her happy. It was alive and fun and suited the cottage. She'd gotten some nice kitchen knobs at the hardware store, just simple rounds of pewter color, but when she held one up, she knew it was a huge improvement over the old chipped wooden ones. In fact, it looked perfect! Who knew hard work could actually be this fun? But now it was time to call it a day and throw some dinner together. The lower cabinets would have to wait.

Since the kitchen was so chaotic, Wendy suggested they roast hot dogs in the fireplace, and Jackson was more than happy to make a fire. Even with the disarray all around them, Wendy couldn't help but notice how cozy it all felt. It would be hard to leave this behind.

The next morning, they both went back to work. Jackson was determined to finish his room and put it back together, and Wendy wanted to paint the rest of the cabinets. As she steadily worked, she lost track of the time and was surprised when Jackson announced it was almost time to go to town.

"What?" She looked up from painting.

"To help Caleb put up lights." He grabbed Oliver's leash. "I'll take him out for a quick run, but we should go pretty soon."

It was hard to stop painting with only one cabinet left, but when Jackson and Oliver came back, she set down her brush and got her keys.

"My room is all done," Jackson bragged as they got in the car.

"Good job."

"Can you believe how much we've accomplished in such a short time?"

"We're way ahead of schedule."

"What schedule?"

"Oh, I don't know . . ." She considered this as she drove. Was it time to tell him of her plan to list the cottage with a Realtor? But they were close to town—and she thought it was unfair to spring bad news right before she dropped him off.

"Do you mean before Christmas?" he persisted.

"We definitely want to be done before Christmas. But you know we're getting it ready to sell, Jackson. I've told you—"

"But we'll be here for Christmas," he insisted. "We have to be here for Christmas, Mom. And you don't know what might happen after that. Remember, you promised to trust God."

"Well, at any rate, it would be nice to have it mostly wrapped up by next week. And I think it's possible." She tossed an uneasy glance his way. His obstinate denial was hard to deal with. Especially when he threw God into the mix. But what if he came home one day to see a FOR SALE sign in the yard? Would that be enough to convince him they couldn't stay here? Still, this wasn't the time for a painful reality check. "So, you never told me what you thought about the paint color in your room."

"I love it. It's perfect. Almost exactly what I'd been imagining."

"I can't wait to see it." She turned toward town.

"But remember you promised not to look until I put it all back together again. Remember?"

"Yes, I remember."

"And no cheating when you go back home."

"No cheating." She pulled up to Caleb's shop just as he came out the door carrying a red plastic box.

"Hey, you're right on time," he said as Jackson hopped out.

"Reporting for duty." Jackson made a mock salute.

"Take this." Caleb handed him the box, then leaned in the still-opened door. "Are you sticking around or—"

"No way." She held up her paint-splotched hands. "I have to go home and finish a project, but I can pick him—"

"Why not just let Jackson stay until five? We'll meet you at the town square."

"Okay." She nodded. "Thanks."

"Mom, will you bring Oliver?" Jackson called over Caleb's shoulder. "Please!"

"Oliver?" Caleb looked confused—or maybe concerned.

"Jackson's dog," she told him. "Remember?"

He chuckled. "Oh, yeah." He turned to Jackson. "I'd like to meet this guy."

"Is it okay to bring him for the celebration?" Jackson asked hopefully.

"Sure, lots of people bring their dogs. Seaside is a very dog-friendly town. Well, as long as the dogs are people-friendly."

"Oliver is really friendly," Jackson assured him.

"Then you should definitely bring him." Caleb grinned at Wendy.

Knowing she was stuck, Wendy reluctantly agreed.

"Thanks!" Jackson's whole face lit up.

"See you at five." She tried to hide her annoyance at being shanghaied by the two of them as she waved and drove away. On one hand, it was sort of sweet. But on the other hand, it was only going to make it harder when she eventually told Jackson that Oliver had to find a new home. But maybe Caleb wanted a dog.

It took her about an hour to finish up the kitchen cabinets, and as she stepped back to take in the whole thing, she couldn't help but smile. Sure, it might not be for everyone, but she felt it was turning into a very pretty kitchen. Even the old white laminate countertop looked better next to the freshly painted cabinets. And with some careful staging with the Fiestaware dishes and a few charming beach items, it would be absolutely perfect.

As she cleaned herself up, Wendy felt more hopeful than she'd been in a long time. Things were getting done and lining up—maybe after the past few years of heartache and disappointment, she and Jackson were finally about to get ahead in life. Maybe even by Christmas. It felt like God was finally smiling down upon them—like there was a light at the end of their long, dark tunnel. Sure, maybe the glow wasn't shining here in Seaside . . . but it was out there somewhere.

# Eleven

WENDY DUG AROUND in the pile of clothes that she still hadn't hung back in her closet after painting her bedroom. She wanted something festive and fun to wear to tonight's celebration, but knowing it was getting pretty chilly out, she decided to go for warmth. Remembering the old sweater she'd salvaged from a pile of clothes in the storage room, she decided to give it a try. She suspected the fisherman knit cardigan had been Poppa's since it looked too big for her petite grandmother. Slipping it on, she immediately loved the oversized garment, which had softened with age. And it actually looked rather stylish with her best jeans and favorite pair of dark brown boots. To dress it up, she added a red plaid scarf around her neck, as well as some silver earrings. Nothing fancy, but suitable, she felt, for Seaside. And instead of her usual no-nonsense ponytail, she brushed out her long dark hair and let it hang loose.

She was about to leave when she remembered her promise to Jackson regarding Oliver. She'd found a bag of old red and blue bandanas, which she planned to recycle into curtains and accents in Jackson's room, and decided to utilize one now. Oliver didn't even mind as she tied a red one around his neck, then hooked up his new red leash. "Aren't you a pretty boy?" she said as he leaped up into the back of the car. She continued to talk to him as she drove to town. "You'll probably be the life of the party," she said as she let him out. "Well, as long as you mind your manners. If you don't, I'll bring you straight back to the car."

But Oliver didn't look the least concerned as she led him down Main Street. He walked right next to her as if he'd been trained. And with his jaunty red bandana and tail held high, Wendy couldn't help but smile as they got closer to the city square where people were gathered for the tree-lighting ceremony.

"You brought him!" Jackson exclaimed as he and Caleb joined her. "And you even dressed him up." He hugged her then took the leash. "Thanks, Mom!"

"Nice-looking dog you got there." Caleb grinned at her. "And you're not so bad either."

"Thanks . . . I think." A warm rush ran through her at his offhanded compliment.

"Come on." He grabbed her hand. "I've got a place saved over there. You can see everything." He led her, Jackson, and Oliver to a concrete retaining wall where a tartan blanket was spread out. "Have a seat." He handed her a paper cup. "Hot cocoa to warm your hands and your tummy."

"Thanks."

"I'm going back for another cookie," Jackson told Wendy. "You guys want some? They have ginger cookies, Mom."

"That sounds great!"

"I'll take one too," Caleb said.

With cocoa in hand, Wendy sat on the blanket, then turned to Caleb. "Thanks for telling us about this. It's really fun."

"Small-town life can grow on you." He sat next to her. "There was a time when I thought I needed the big city, but it didn't take too long before I figured out there was no place like home."

She smiled. "So you clicked your heels together?"

"Something like that." He nodded to the stage where musicians were starting to play "Deck the Halls." "That's the Seaside High band. Not very big, but the band director is pretty talented. He gets the best out of these kids."

"They sound good."

"The dance team will do a number and then, after some speeches and hoopla, Santa will show up and push the magical button that will light up the tree." He pointed to the tall evergreen next to the stage.

"How exciting!" she said with mock enthusiasm.

"Shortly after that happens, I have to make a sprint back to my store and get ready to turn on my Christmas lights. Santa will introduce the Sugar Plum Fairy, and when that dance is over, Santa will push another magic button and the whole town will light up at exactly 5:30. Or thereabouts. Not everyone's watches are perfectly synchronized."

"Amazing." She grinned.

"Yes, it's all rather magical." He took a sip of cocoa. "Same thing every year, but the crowd loves it. After everything is all lit up, we sing carols and eat cookies for a while. And that's it." He glanced up at the sky. "Sometimes it's freezing cold or snowing and we don't last too long. But tonight's not so bad." He touched her sweater sleeve. "Hope that's as warm as it looks."

"It is." She explained how she found it. "I think it was my grandpa's."

"Well, it looks great on you."

Jackson was coming back with Oliver as well as Taylor and a smaller girl in tow. As Jackson doled out their cookies, Taylor introduced them to her little sister, Tessa. "Mom dropped us off before she went to work," she explained. "I told her that maybe we could get a ride home with Jackson." Her smile was a mixture of hope and mischief.

"Of course, we'll give you girls a ride," Wendy assured her. "No problem."

"Great." Taylor grinned. "And can Tessa stay with you guys while Jackson and I go over there to talk to our friends?"

Wendy wasn't sure what to say, but seeing that the little girl was shivering, she agreed. "You look cold," she told Tessa. "Let's get you up here." She bent down to help, but before she could, Caleb swooped the little girl up, setting her between them on the retaining wall.

"We'll all snuggle up next to you," he told Tessa. "That should keep you warm."

"Have you been to the lighting celebration before?" Wendy asked Tessa, lifting up the back of the blanket like a shawl on the little girl's back.

"No." Tessa shook her head.

"Did you know that Santa's supposed to show up here tonight?" Caleb asked.

"Really?" Tessa's eyes grew wide.

"He's the one who makes everything light up," Caleb told her.

"Can I talk to him?" Tessa asked hopefully.

Wendy looked over her head to Caleb. "Can she?" she mouthed.

"For sure. All the kids are invited to visit with Santa afterward," he assured Tessa. "The smart kids get in line before the celebration is over."

"Can I do that too?" she asked.

"You bet," Wendy told her. The music grew louder, and then, just like clockwork, the program unfolded pretty much as Caleb had described. After the tree burst into light, amid cheers and applause, Caleb slipped away. The Sugar Plum Fairy did her dance and Santa pushed the next "magic button." Everyone watched as the whole darkened town lit up—from the gas station clear down to the docks—with thousands of lights. It was so beautiful that it literally took Wendy's breath away. She was tempted to pull out her phone and attempt some photos, but she didn't want to spoil the moment with electronics. Better to just enjoy it for what it was. Who knew if she'd ever see it again?

Shortly after Caleb returned, while they were singing carols, Wendy noticed some of the smaller children already lining up near Santa's sled. "Let's go," she whispered to Tessa. "Time to see Santa." As they waited in line, Wendy spotted Jackson and Taylor, along with several other kids their age. Oliver, looking dapper in his red bandana, appeared to be the center of attention. It was fun seeing Jackson smiling and socializing—having a good time. In fact, the scene was so sweet and wholesome that it nearly brought tears to Wendy's eyes. She understood why Jackson loved this place. If only . . .

"Jackson probably didn't get a chance to tell you that he accepted my invitation for dinner," Caleb told her while Tessa climbed onto Santa's lap.

She blinked. "You're taking Jackson to dinner?"

"He accepted for *both* of you." Caleb grinned. "He mentioned your kitchen was a mess and that cooking might be a challenge tonight."

"Maybe, but I think we can work it out." She nodded toward Tessa. "Besides I promised to give the girls a ride and—"

"Go ahead and take them home. Then you and Jackson can swing over to my place. It's not too far from where you live."

"You know where I live?"

"Seaside is a small world, Wendy." He winked. "Besides Jackson told me."

"Sounds like my son told you a lot."

"As a matter of fact, he did. He also told me that you like seafood."

"That's true." It was also true that, since she'd only had an apple for lunch, she was ravenous. Not that she planned to admit to it. Instead, she thanked him, accepting the invite. He told her where he lived, less than a mile from the cottage, just as Tessa's Santa visit wrapped up. Wendy was imagining prawns and oysters and salmon as she delivered Tessa and Taylor home, but by the time she stopped at the cottage to drop off the dog, Jackson pulled the plug on her daydream.

"I really don't want to leave Oliver home alone," he informed her. They were on the front porch, waiting for the dog to do his "business" in the yard. "And I doubt the restaurant allows dogs."

"He'll be just fine on his own," she assured him.

"I don't know, Mom. I mean he's still getting used to us. He might feel left out. Like Taylor says, he's probably got some abandonment issues."

She tried not to laugh. "Just feed him, tell him you love him, and that you'll be home before long. Trust me, he'll probably sleep the whole time we're gone."

"Maybe . . . But that's not all. I need to put my room back together. My bed and my stuff are still piled at the top of the stairs. I'd rather just stay home."

Wendy envisioned her delicious seafood dinner going up in a puff of smoke. "Then I better call Caleb and tell him we can't make—"

"No—you should go, Mom. Caleb will be disappointed if we both bail on him."

"But you need some dinner and—"

"I'll fix myself something to eat. And Caleb will understand. I'll feel guilty if you don't go because of me."

"But I don't—"

"*Please, Mom.* Just go have some dinner with him. I'll feel better if you do."

"Well, I won't promise anything, but since I don't have his phone number, I better at least go tell him what's up." She opened the front door, reminding Jackson to lock up. As she drove the short distance to Caleb's house, she was determined to beg out on dinner tonight. But when she found his place, one of the older beach cabins and similar to hers, Caleb opened the door with a wide smile.

"Dinner is almost ready."

She felt confused. "What do you mean?"

"Chef Caleb at your service." He led her inside, where the smell of something delicious wafted toward her. "I got lobster, crab, mussels, and shrimp down at the dock this morning. I'm making a big pot of seafood stew." He peered out the door. "Where's Jackson?"

She explained about Jackson's concern for Oliver. "So I was going to ask for a rain check." She sniffed the air. "But that smells so good . . . I don't know."

"Jackson can bring Oliver over here." Caleb waved a hand toward the spacious great room. "This place is dog-friendly. Call him and insist that he come."

As she retrieved her phone, Wendy surveyed the attractive room. Gleaming wood floors, open-beam ceilings, a big stone fireplace, large leather sectional, and several pieces of handcrafted wood furnishings. "What a gorgeous room."

"Thank you."

"Looks like you've done some major remodeling." She pushed speed dial. "From the outside it looks similar to my cottage, but inside . . . well, it's completely different. Really beautiful."

"Yeah, I took out some walls to open it up."

Jackson answered and she quickly relayed Caleb's invitation for Oliver. "I can come get you and—"

"I just made a big turkey sandwich and—"

"But you could save it for—"

"You stay and eat with Caleb, Mom. Oliver and I are fine at home. Besides, I'm kinda tired. I might go to bed early, you know, after I get my room together."

She persisted a bit more, but knew by his tone that his mind was made up. As she put away her phone, she grew suspicious. Was this simply a ploy? Had Jackson schemed for her to have dinner *alone* with Caleb? Since when did he want to go to bed early? She wondered if Caleb was involved.

"Jackson wants to stay home," she said as she joined Caleb in the kitchen. "And now I'm starting to think that something is fishy."

Caleb laughed. "You mean besides my stew?"

She studied his expression as she unbuttoned her heavy cardigan. "It feels almost like a setup. Did you have anything to do with it?"

Caleb looked innocently at her. "*Moi?*"

She frowned, but decided not to obsess as she studied his updated kitchen. Concrete countertops, gorgeous wood cabinets, and appliances that were state-of-the-art. "Are you a serious cook?" she asked.

"Serious?" He shrugged. "I like good food. As a bachelor, I don't like eating out all the time. So I taught myself to cook." He pointed to the big pot where all the wonderful smells were coming from. "This is Nana's seafood stew recipe, been in the family for generations." He held up a loaf of artisan bread and a bottle of sparkling cider. "You add these ingredients and you have a simple but delicious meal."

She glanced over to the dining area, relieved to see that three place settings were already on the beautiful live-edge table. "I guess we won't need this." She picked up one of the settings, placing it on the counter. "So maybe you and Jackson didn't scheme after all." She smiled. "Forgive my suspicions."

Caleb chuckled as he sliced the bread. "Well, it was a natural assumption. And I'm probably not above a bit of manipulation when it comes to getting a date with you."

"So this *is* a date?"

He laughed. "Call it whatever you like, Wendy. But the stew is ready. Want to bring those bowls over here?"

Before long they were enjoying what was probably the best meal she'd had in years. Whether it was the good food or the good company, she could tell her guard was going down.

But the more they visited, the more she realized that Caleb knew more about her than she knew of him.

"Sounds like you've been doing your research," she said as he set a second bowl of fisherman's stew before her.

"Jackson's a good conversationalist."

"But it puts me at a disadvantage. Or maybe I should interrogate my son about you."

"I'm pretty much an open book. If you want to know anything—just ask away."

"I do have one question . . . How is it that a guy like you—a superb cook who lives in a gorgeous home—has not been snatched up by now?" She studied him closely.

He shrugged. "Well, it's not that I haven't had opportunity."

"Obviously. I mean, I've seen Crystal."

He wrinkled his nose. "She's not my type."

"What is your type?"

His eyes twinkled. "What do *you* think?"

She felt her cheeks grow warm. "I think the rumors I've heard are true."

"What rumors?"

"That you're a confirmed bachelor."

He laughed. "Maybe so."

"So are you saying you've never met a woman who was your type?"

"No, I'm not saying that." He took another piece of bread. "There was someone."

"Aha." She nodded. "Tell me more."

"Maggie Stewart." His tone grew wistful. "She was a local girl. Very sweet and pretty. The kind of person who could light up a room when she entered. To be honest, she was my first love, but I was pretty shy back then. And Maggie Stewart was so popular and so sure of herself . . . well, I knew she was out of my league—so I sort of worshiped her from afar."

"And?"

"Anyway, Maggie's family used to own a furniture store—"

"Stewart's Fine Furnishings," Wendy supplied. "My grandma bought a recliner there. It's still in the house . . . well, at least for a while. I plan to let it go soon."

"Maggie worked there after school and in the summers. And I worked at She Sells sometimes. That's sort of how we first became friends—when we were both seventeen. She was so outgoing that she went after me. I could hardly believe it. By our senior year, we were dating pretty steadily, and after graduation, we both went to UNE . . . and we continued dating." He got a sad, faraway look, and Wendy regretted pushing him. She suspected that the popular young woman had found someone else and broken his heart. Maybe it was still painful.

"So it ended badly?" she finally said. "You both went your separate ways?"

"Sort of. She died in a car wreck shortly before college graduation."

"Oh . . . I'm so sorry."

He barely nodded. "We were engaged by then, planning to get married that summer. I was totally devastated by her death. That's when I decided to take a job in New York. I guess I hoped to lose myself in the big city. But after a few years, I got homesick for Seaside and a quieter life. I'd always loved woodworking, so Nana encouraged me to start my own business and helped me get set up. And I've just been working really hard ever since. I had some pretty lean years early on—after the economy tanked. But it's steadily picked up. I guess my best excuse for not having been snatched up, as you say, was that I've been too busy. Oh, I've dated now and then. Friends and family are always trying to set me up. But the right woman just never came along."

For a long moment, neither of them spoke. Then Wendy broke the silence. "Well, I know how hard it is to lose someone you love," she said quietly. "And I appreciate you sharing your story with me, Caleb."

He changed the conversation to happier things, asking about her cottage renovations and giving her some useful tips for bringing the pine floor in the kitchen back to life. As she helped him clean up after dinner, Wendy was surprised at how relaxed and comfortable she felt with him now. Familiar . . . and good. But it was also a bit disconcerting. She wasn't used to feeling like this—or being alone with a man in his home.

As she dried her hands on the kitchen towel, Caleb set something in the sink. She turned to see him gazing at her with a look she hadn't seen in a long time. "I, uh, I probably should go," she said. "Jackson is home alone and I, uh . . ."

He moved closer to her. Like a magnet, she moved toward him, and the next instant they were embracing and kissing—right there in his kitchen! When they finally stepped apart, she felt breathless and speechless . . . and embarrassed.

"I'm sorry," he said. "I hadn't planned that."

"Me either." She hung up the towel. "I, uh, I really should go."

"Yeah, it's getting late."

"I hate to eat and run." She moved away, putting the breakfast bar between them. "But I really don't like leaving Jackson home alone for too long."

"I understand." He nodded with a solemn expression. "You're a good mom."

She shrugged. "Not as good as I wish." Thoughts of how she'd misled Jackson pressed in on her.

"No one's as good as they'd like. It's just part of the human condition."

"I suppose that's true." She pulled on her sweater.

"Speaking of the human condition"—he followed her to the front door—"I invited Jackson to church tomorrow, and he sounded interested. The youth group is supposed to be pretty good." While he walked her to her car, he gave her the specifics. Still feeling a little off balance, she thanked him and left. As she drove the short distance home, she daydreamed about Caleb—wondering if he was what could keep her and Jackson in Seaside. Or had she read more into this evening than he'd intended? After all, he'd practically admitted he was a confirmed bachelor. As she parked her car in front of the cottage, she reminded herself that dreams didn't usually come true. At least not for her. Better to focus on reality—and just make the best of it.

# Twelve

I LIKE CALEB'S CHURCH," Jackson said as Wendy drove them home. "The youth group is pretty cool. I want to ask Taylor to come next week."

"That'd be nice." Wendy wanted to remind Jackson that next week might be their last Sunday here. She planned to call a Realtor in the next few days, hopefully list the cottage by next weekend . . . and go home. But the words got stuck in her throat.

"Speaking of Taylor!" Jackson leaned forward, pointing to a girl walking on the side of the road with a shopping bag. "Can we give her a ride?"

"Sure." She pulled over.

"Where you going?" Jackson asked as Taylor hopped in.

"Home. I just walked to the store."

"That's a long walk," Wendy said.

"I know. Almost five miles round trip. But Mom was asleep, and we were out of milk and cereal. I would've ridden my bike, but it's got a flat."

Wendy felt sorry for Taylor but didn't know what to say. She'd barely met Taylor's mom, but could see Kara struggled to make ends meet. It wasn't easy being a single mom in a seasonal tourist town. Wendy understood.

"My uncle's taking Tessa and me to get a Christmas tree later," Taylor said. "We're gonna go out into the woods and cut one down ourselves. I mean a wild one, not like from a tree farm. Uncle Greg is a logger so he knows how to do it."

"Cool," Jackson said.

"Uncle Greg said there's a big storm coming and we gotta get our tree this weekend because there could be a lot of snow by next weekend."

"Really? A big storm?" Wendy pulled in front of Taylor's house. "Do you get snow here on the coast?"

"I guess so. Anyway, that's what Uncle Greg says. We didn't live here last year." She reached over the front seat to nudge Jackson. "Wanna come with us, Jackson? You could bring Oliver too. It'd be fun."

"Can I go, Mom?" he asked.

"Well, I—"

"Please," he begged.

Wendy reluctantly agreed, and Taylor told Jackson to be at her house before one. "And wear warm clothes and tough shoes," Taylor told him. "That's what Uncle Greg told us."

When it was time to go to Taylor's house, Jackson looked well prepared, but when he started to go, Wendy grabbed her coat and insisted on walking with him. "I want to meet Taylor's uncle," she explained as they walked against the wind. She wasn't even sure that this "Uncle Greg" was really an uncle. For all she knew, he might be Kara's boyfriend. Sometimes moms called boyfriends "uncles."

"Oh, Mom."

"I'm sorry," she said. "Call me overprotective, but I'm not

letting my only son go off with a complete stranger." She didn't admit that she'd been imagining what could've been a scene from a Stephen King novel, where some toothless guy with a beer belly and a broken-down pickup carted away her precious son. "And just so you know, if I don't feel good about him, you can't go."

He grumbled even louder now. But to her relief, Greg appeared to be a respectable guy. He politely introduced his wife, Lori, confirming that he was indeed Kara's brother, and exchanged phone numbers with her. "I'm the reason Kara and the girls moved here." He opened up the back door to the crew cab pickup, waiting as his nieces scrambled in. "I felt like Taylor and Tess needed some family in their lives."

Jackson gave her an I-told-you-so look as he and Oliver climbed into the backseat with the girls. Satisfied that her son was safe, Wendy waved goodbye and hurried back home. Her plan was to get the kitchen put back together and a few other things done. Hopefully she'd get everything wrapped up by the end of the week—and call a Realtor.

A couple of hours later, Wendy stepped back to admire her "new" kitchen curtains. She'd up-cycled white pillowcases with hand-crocheted lace trim for in here and in her bedroom. And the recycled vintage linens looked perfectly charming—if she did say so herself. She was just closing them when she noticed Greg's pickup pull into her driveway. The next thing she knew, Jackson, with Greg's help, was hauling a large evergreen tree into the living room.

"What have you—"

"Greg let me get a tree too," Jackson declared. "I cut it down myself."

"Merry Christmas!" Greg called out. "Enjoy!"

"But we don't even have a tree stand or ornaments," Wendy helplessly told Jackson. "And it's so big, where will we put—"

"Greg told me to wedge it in a big bucket with some stones and just fill it with water." He pointed to the wall adjacent to the fireplace. "How about right there?"

Wendy was speechless. Of course, Jackson assumed they'd be here for Christmas. Somehow she needed to straighten him out.

"Don't worry, Mom. I'll get it all set up. Just trust me."

"But I need to paint that wall first," she protested. "And I didn't plan to start on it until tomorrow or the next day."

"I'll paint it. Right now, if you want." He smiled brightly. "I like to paint!"

"Well, you did a great job on your room." She'd been really impressed. Not only did the paint look good, he'd arranged the furniture nicely too. Almost like he knew it needed to be staged. So she agreed he could paint while she fixed dinner.

By the time Wendy announced bedtime, the pine tree, now wedged in a five-gallon bucket, stood proudly next to the freshly painted wall. "It looks really good." Wendy hugged Jackson. "Nice work."

"Thanks." He stifled a yawn and called out to the dog, already snoozing on the rug by the fireplace. "Time for bed, Oliver."

The next morning, Wendy got up before the sun. She had a lot to get done this week. So much, in fact, that she sat down at the kitchen table to make a long list. Her goal was to get the house thoroughly cleaned, complete the painting, and attractively stage it—by Friday. Then she'd call a Realtor and try to have it listed for the next weekend. All of that sounded easy compared to breaking the news to Jackson. But she was determined to do it this morning. Her plan was to invite him to do some beachcombing . . . and then when they were at least twenty minutes from home, she would gently break the news. She knew he'd be upset, but hopefully on the walk back to the cottage, he'd have a chance to cool down and listen to reason.

Although she'd protected him in the past, it was time for him to grasp their financial situation. As delightful as Seaside was, she could not afford to live here without a steady source of income. And without selling the cottage, she would never climb out from beneath her load of debt. Even with their social security pittance, she still needed full-time, year-round employment with benefits, which was practically nonexistent in Seaside. Selling the cottage was the only real option. She had to make him understand.

Hearing him clomping down the stairs, chatting cheerfully with Oliver, she folded her to-do list and slipped it into the back pocket of her jeans. "Good morning," she told Jackson. "You're up early."

"Because it's *Monday*." He took Oliver to the laundry room, pouring kibble into his bowl.

"I know it's Monday." She frowned. "So?"

"So it's a school day." He opened the fridge, taking out the milk.

"A school day?" She blinked.

"Yeah." He poured a glass of milk. "And the bus will be here in about five minutes. I forgot to set the alarm on my phone." He downed the milk then reached for an apple. "This is all I have time for this morning."

"But Jackson—what do you mean? How is it you're going to school?"

"Mom." He took a bite of the apple as he pulled on his jacket. "I'm a kid. That's what we do. Remember?" He grinned as he loudly chewed.

"But how do you—"

"Taylor told me about the bus, which will be here any minute. Can I have some lunch money?"

"But you have to be registered," she said anxiously, "and I'd have to go with you and sign things and—"

"Nope." He shook his head, still chewing as he handed her purse to her. "When Taylor's mom took Tessa to the grade school, Taylor went to the middle school by herself. She said it's really easy. You just go to the office and give 'em your social security number and the name of your previous school and some other stuff. Then bring home papers for your mom to sign. No big deal."

"But I don't—"

"Hurry, Mom." He pulled out her wallet for her. "Taylor said lunch is around three bucks, but we can probably get on the free program—if we're poor enough." He reached into her wallet to extract three dollars. "Thanks!" He pointed to the window. "There's the bus. I gotta go. Taylor said she'd tell them to stop for me." Just like that, he shot out the door and raced down the driveway where a big yellow bus hissed to a stop, swallowed him, and chugged off toward town.

Wendy sank into a kitchen chair. This wasn't happening! It couldn't be happening. What was she going to do? She felt sick inside. She'd allowed this to go too far. Way too far. It was like she was getting buried alive in this town. Somehow, she had to dig them out. She refilled her coffee cup and tried to think.

As she stared out the window toward the foggy beach, it slowly came to her. Why not let Jackson go to school for a few days? She could use that time to get the house ready, have the Realtor over . . . and then when it was time to put the FOR SALE sign in the yard, she would tell him. Okay, it wasn't a fabulous plan, but it was all she had at the moment. And after procrastinating this long, what difference would a few more days make?

So, instead of sitting around in a pool of pity, Wendy rolled up her sleeves and opened a paint can. It was time to finish up the painting—with no distractions. Well, except for a dog.

But she came to realize, after a couple of days of quietly working, that Oliver was actually fairly low-maintenance. Other than his food and water and an occasional walk, he was pretty easygoing. And to her surprise, he was good company.

"It's not that I don't like you," she told Oliver as she drove to town on Tuesday afternoon. "I really do. It's just that I don't know what we're going to do with you when it's time to go to Ohio. I'd really like for you to find a good home." With the cottage in pretty good shape, she had four tasks to accomplish—go to the hardware store for some final tweaking items, get some groceries, find a reliable Realtor, and stop by the vet clinic.

She decided to tackle the hardest chore first, going directly to the veterinarian where she'd earlier posted a "found dog" notice—that had gotten no response. Today she would post a "free dog" poster on the bulletin board. Without access to a printer, she'd relied on her own artistic talents to draw a sketch of Oliver, complete with red bandana. But as she returned to the car, where Oliver was happily waiting for her, she felt like a traitor. In a perfect world, she would gladly keep the dog. But unfortunately, her world was less than perfect.

Her next hardest task was to find a good Realtor. She started with a well-located office, the sort of a place where a visitor might make an inquiry. She went in and spoke to a receptionist, giving her some general information about the cottage. "Sandi Atkins is who you need," the receptionist said as she wrote down Wendy's phone number. "She'll call you as soon as she gets back from the dentist. I happen to know she's got a cash buyer looking for a property just like that."

"Really?"

"Yes. If it's as nice as it sounds, your house could be sold in no time." The woman smiled. "Sandi should be back here in about an hour."

"If she can't call before three, I'd prefer she call tomorrow morning."

The receptionist made note of that, and then Wendy left for the hardware store. Not only did she find all the items on her list, she also got a couple strands of white Christmas tree lights. So far they'd been simply enjoying the tree in its natural form, but she knew Jackson wanted it lit. Perhaps it would help cheer him up—after she broke the news. Finally she went to the grocery store, where she had to shop carefully since her cash was running low. Still, the hope that there could be a cash buyer out there—that the house could be sold within days—well, it almost made her want to celebrate. Or cry.

Back at the cottage, Wendy opened the front door and, letting Oliver go inside, pretended to be a buyer here to see the house. The living room, with all its walls painted and windows scrubbed, looked fresh and clean. The wood floors, though worn, were gleaming, and the thinned-down furnishings helped the room appear larger. She still didn't have any window coverings in here, but with the open view of the ocean, she thought perhaps it was better.

She frowned at the bare tree. It would be more appealing if it was decorated, although she had no ornaments or cash to spend on some. She carried her groceries into the kitchen, wondering if there was something she could bake and hang on the tree. But seeing her nearly finished shell-framed mirror project still on the table, it hit her—she had shells! Not only did she have about a hundred beautiful white sand dollars, she had all sorts of other shells too. She would make shell ornaments for the tree.

She put her groceries away, then got out a box of sand dollars and began to play until she came up with a simple design. Before long, she was hot-gluing two clam shells onto a sand dollar, like wings, and using a piece of sea glass for a head—to make what resembled an angel—a little white sea angel. By the time her phone jangled she had made a dozen.

"Hello?" Wendy answered cheerfully.

"Good afternoon. I'm Sandi Atkins," a pleasant voice said. "I hear you might be interested in listing a beach cottage."

"Yes—yes, I am." Wendy described her cottage, painting a pretty picture that she hoped wasn't an exaggeration.

"It sounds wonderful. And I think I know exactly which cottage you're referring to. When can I come see it?"

Wendy looked at the kitchen clock that she'd decorated with seashells. "I'm not ready to do this today." She quickly explained that her son didn't know how soon she wanted to sell the cottage. "I want to break it to him gently."

"I understand."

"And the house isn't completely ready to be seen, I mean by a buyer. I want to finish staging it and—"

"Oh, these buyers won't care about staging or even if it's painted."

Wendy felt disappointed. "Well, I care, and I'd like to finish what I started. I've always heard you get a higher price if the house looks better."

"That's generally true. But because there are no other beach cottages like yours on the market, you should get a very fair price."

"Oh?" Wendy considered this. "So you're saying this is a sellers' market?"

"For you it is."

"Well, that's great. How about if you come by in a couple of days? I think I can have it ready by Friday."

"Friday is fine. I'll be optimistic and bring a realty contract with me."

"Okay." Wendy felt a sudden rush of nerves. Was she really doing this?

"I look forward to meeting you on Friday, Wendy."

As she set down her phone, Wendy felt like someone had just knocked the wind out of her sails. Even her previously charming angels no longer interested her. Jackson would soon be home, and it was time to tell him. But how? To calm herself, Wendy decided to make an attempt at decorating the tree. First she strung the lights and then she hung her twelve sea angels. The effect was actually rather charming, but the big tree was in need of more ornaments, and she knew that pretty seashells, as well as more angels, would do the trick.

She was just going for another box of sand dollars when

she heard Oliver barking in the kitchen, followed by the sound of young voices. "Mom!" Jackson called out. "I brought Taylor and Tessa home. Can we have a snack?"

"I'm in here," she called back. Suddenly the three kids and dog burst into the living room.

"You put lights on my tree!" Jackson exclaimed. "It looks great. And angels! Wow, Mom, these are super cool. Did you make them?"

"Yes. And I'm about to make more. Maybe you kids could help."

"Taylor and I want to go clamming," Jackson told her.

"Clamming? In December?"

"Uncle Greg said he got clams just a few days ago," Taylor explained. "I promised Mom I'd try to get some."

"And I've always wanted to dig clams," Jackson told Wendy.

"Then you should go for it." Wendy nodded.

"But Tessa doesn't want to," Taylor said. "It's pretty windy and cold out there. Do you think she could stay with you until we get back?"

"Maybe *you'd* like to make some sand dollar angels," she said to Tessa.

"Yeah." She nodded with wide eyes. "I wanna do that."

"I do too," Jackson assured her. "After we're done clamming."

"Me too," Taylor said.

"Well, I hope you two don't get frozen out there." Wendy looked out the big window. "The weatherman says that nor'easter won't be here until next week."

"Cool." Jackson's eyes lit up. "I wanna see that."

"Maybe we'll have a white Christmas," Taylor said hopefully.

Wendy cringed to think of a snowy drive back to Ohio. Her Subaru was a good winter car, but it really needed snow tires. Then again, if her cash buyers came through, she could easily afford new tires . . . or even a few nights at a really nice hotel. So much would change for her and Jackson once this cottage was sold.

"Hey, are these wings made from clam shells?" Taylor pointed to an angel.

"Yes. And if you see any clam shells on the beach, be sure to bring them back. I could use some more."

"I see those all the time. We'll bring back lots," Taylor assured her.

"Now can we have a snack?" Jackson asked.

"Yes, of course. I just got groceries so there's plenty to choose from in there. Why don't you take care of your guests, Jackson?"

"Sure." He nodded. "Thanks, Mom."

While Jackson and the girls flocked into the kitchen, Wendy suddenly remembered her "cash buyer." Hurrying out to the car to retrieve the bags from the hardware store, she was determined to wrap up the final fix-ups on her list. This cottage would look as good as possible when Sandi came. Maybe the buyers wouldn't care if all the light switch covers and drawer knobs and miscellaneous hardware matched, but Wendy did. She wanted top dollar for this property. But as far as telling Jackson today . . . well, that would have to wait. Again.

# *Thirteen*

B Y WEDNESDAY AFTERNOON, Wendy had a whole army of angels and several other attractive shell items spread out around the house. And feeling rather clever and innovative, she had an idea. It was probably a long shot, but she thought it was worth a try. Especially for Jackson's sake—she saw how much he loved his new school. What if she really could make a living in Seaside? What if Caleb was right about the potential in selling beach-style home décor items?

The things she'd created so far looked just as nice—maybe nicer—than those in the catalogues. She carefully set the mirror she'd labored over into a large box. The frame was a pleasant combination of interesting seashells, pretty stones, small pieces of smooth driftwood, and even a few sand dollars.

She'd planned to take this mirror back to Ohio with them. But if she could sell it, along with her other creations—and this was the long shot—perhaps it would be enough to keep her and Jackson in Seaside! She laid a tea towel over the mirror, layering a number of sand dollar angels and another tea towel. Not wanting to overwhelm Caleb, she'd decided against taking in all her recently made items, but she had taken photos and felt certain he'd be impressed. As she drove to town she felt hopeful. Even so, she said a prayer.

Her hope diminished slightly when she realized Caleb's shop was closed. But seeing that She Sells Sea Shells was open, she decided to give that a try. Hopefully Ashley was in. Ashley had good taste and might appreciate Wendy's craftsmanship. Wendy was barely through the door when she spied Crystal behind the counter. Ready to make a quick getaway, she turned to leave.

"Wendy." Crystal's tone was flat but too loud to ignore.

"Hey, Crystal." Wendy grimaced.

"What can I do for you?"

"I, uh, I was hoping to see Caleb."

"Weren't we all." Crystal emerged from behind the counter. As usual, her appearance was impeccable. "Caleb is on a business trip. Didn't he mention that to you?"

"Come to think of it, he did say he hoped to deliver the dining room set this week. Is that what he's doing?"

"Yes." Crystal's mouth twisted to one side. "I know that you're interested in him, Wendy. I mean, most of the single women in town are." She laughed, but not in a friendly way. "So it's only fair to tell you that he's pretty much a confirmed bachelor."

"So I've heard."

"He's more married to his business than anything else."

"Yes, I know."

"Well, it only seemed fair for you to know." Crystal pointed to the box in Wendy's arms with a bored expression. "What have you got there? Not peddling your wares again, are you?"

"It was just something to show Caleb." Wendy backed away.

"Let's see." Crystal removed the tea towel and made what looked like a smug smirk. "Well now, what have we here?"

"Those are Christmas ornaments," Wendy said stiffly.

"Did little children make these?" She picked one up, frowning at it.

"Actually, some were made by kids."

"And did you honestly think we could sell something like this here?" She dangled the angel ornaments from her little finger with a look of total disdain.

"Oh, I didn't know for sure. Although they do look better hanging from a tree with lights and—"

"I'm sorry, but I really don't think Ashley would be interested." She dropped the angel back into the box. "The Coltons, as you've probably noticed"—she waved a hand toward an elegant display of jewelry—"have exquisite taste. And no offense, Wendy, but these seem a little childish." She dropped the towel back onto the box. "Sorry."

Wendy muttered "that's okay" as she hurried from the shop. She suspected that Crystal was not the least bit sorry and that she'd enjoyed embarrassing her. But Crystal was probably right—the sand dollar ornaments really did look childish and out of place in the sleek, stylish shop. Really, what had Wendy been thinking? Thankful that Caleb hadn't been around to see her humiliation—or to deliver his own verdict, which she knew he would've done much more kindly— she got in her car and drove back home with fresh resolve. The cottage had to be sold.

For the next two days, while Jackson was at school, Wendy worked hard to get everything shipshape. The solution to her financial challenges was to stick to her original plan. Sell the cottage, return to Ohio, and be back at her job as promised shortly before Christmas. To that end, she did all she could to make the place sparkle and shine. She even set out the shell items she'd created as accent pieces. And when she was done, she felt the effect was truly charming.

On Friday afternoon, she'd just finished installing the red-and-blue bandana curtains and matching throw cushions in Jackson's room when Sandi Atkins showed up. The cottage, in Wendy's opinion, had never looked better. She almost couldn't believe how much she and Jackson had accomplished with just two weeks and a very meager budget. And for the most part, it was done. As she hurried downstairs to open the front door, she felt a flush of pride.

She greeted Sandi and welcomed her into the house, starting the tour in the living room and explaining about the various improvements she and Jackson had made. Although Sandi was complimentary as she snapped photos, she was also good at pointing out things that still needed a little work. "The fireplace is lovely, but that mantel should be bigger—more prominent." She pointed to the ancestor photos that Jackson had put up there. "And it's usually better not to have family photos around when the buyers are looking. It's a distraction."

"Oh, yes, I know that. My son put those there."

"Do you mind removing them for my photo? I really want to get this fireplace."

"Not at all." Wendy gathered the photos, watching as Sandi shot the room from various angles, primarily focusing on the view of the beach and the fireplace. "They're going to like this."

"And this is the kitchen." Wendy stepped aside, explaining how they discovered original wood floors beneath the old vinyl.

"Nice, but this kitchen countertop is certainly dated,"

Sandi said. "And the space is pretty small. But that won't bother the buyers."

"I know it's old and small, but I think it's kind of charming, you know, in a cottage sort of way." Wendy tried not to sound too defensive. "But maybe that's because I grew up with it." She waved to the turquoise cabinets. "What do you think about this color?"

"Well, it's certainly fun and cheery. I personally like it. And I love those Fiestaware dishes. However, the buyers probably won't like it."

"Oh? I suppose it could be repainted."

"Yes . . . or something." She went to the back door. "What's out there?"

"The laundry porch." Wendy pulled back the curtain. "The dog's out there right now and I haven't really had time to do anything to it . . . yet. But I've been wanting to paint it the same color as the bathroom and—"

"No, no, don't bother with painting it. I'm sure the buyers won't care." She took some more shots of the kitchen. "I love that the kitchen window has an ocean view too. This house is really well placed on this lot. The buyers are going to love that."

"Oh, good." Wendy led her to the refurbished bathroom, explaining about fixing the dry rot.

"This is cute—and it's a nice big bathroom." Sandi took some photos. "But that shower needs to be upgraded. And the floor, well, Carrara marble would've been a good choice."

"Albeit expensive."

"These buyers have deep pockets. And they've been looking for a lovely vacation property for about a year now. This just might work."

Wendy felt confused. If there was so much wrong, how could it work? But she continued the tour just the same, waiting as Sandi took photos and made comments—both good and bad. Good that the house had three bedrooms. Bad that they were so small. "Although I think a master suite could be created on the second floor," she told Wendy. "That would be a great improvement."

Finally they were back in the living room and Sandi looked quite pleased. "I really think this is going to work for them."

"But so much is wrong."

"Yes, but those were fixable things, Wendy." Sandi pulled a contract from her briefcase. "I got this ready—just in case. It's not a sales contract. Just a contract for my agency. Should we go over it now?"

Wendy told her they'd have to finish before Jackson got home, and they sat down and went over it. Wendy was keeping one eye on the clock and trying to pay attention. She was pleasantly surprised by the price Sandi felt was reasonable. "And your buyers are comfortable with that?" she asked. "I mean, in light of all the improvements you think they'd want to do?"

"Absolutely." Sandi smiled. "It's a bit unusual to sell a vacation house in the winter, but these buyers have been looking for a while. I'm sure they'll be delighted to get this purchase tied up in time for Christmas."

Wendy felt a little uneasy as she signed the Realtor contract. But she reminded herself this wasn't the same as selling the house. It was simply the first step. "When do you think the buyers will come see it?"

"I'm hoping this weekend or early next week." Sandi put her copy of the contract back in her briefcase. "Although I hear the weather is going to be rather nasty and they'll be driving from Portland."

"Oh."

"But I'll send them the photos and information—and we'll see what they say." She stood. "Perhaps they'll trust me enough to buy it sight unseen."

"Really?"

"It's entirely possible. The most important thing to them is getting a great location and a solid home that can be improved without changing the footprint. This fits the bill perfectly."

"It's really a sweet old house." Wendy felt a lump in her throat.

"Well, hopefully we'll have it sold within the week." Sandi shook her hand. "How does that sound?"

"Good." Wendy forced a weak smile as she thanked her and walked her outside, waiting as Sandi took yet more photos. "I don't want to rush you," Wendy told her, "but my son will be here soon, and he still doesn't know we're selling this place yet."

"Well, you better tell him by Thursday." Sandi smiled brightly. "Because I'm 99 percent certain this house will be sold." She waved to Wendy and hurried to her car. Wendy watched from the porch as Sandi drove away. She knew she'd made the right and responsible decision, that this was the grown-up thing to do. But why was it so hard to be an adult sometimes?

She was about to go into the house when she heard the hiss of the school bus brakes. Relieved that Sandi was gone, Wendy waved to Jackson as he ran up to the house. He held up his phone. "Caleb sent me a text, Mom."

"Oh?" They went into the house.

"He wants me to help him in his woodshop tomorrow."

"Really?"

Jackson read the message to her, and sure enough, it sounded like he wanted an assistant. "Can I call him back and say yes?"

She shrugged. "I guess so." She waited as Jackson talked to Caleb, and then he handed her the phone. "Hello?"

"I just want to make sure you were okay with this." He explained how he needed a helper to do some hand-sanding on a number of small jobs. "I'm a little overwhelmed with several commissioned projects that need to be finished by Christmas—putting in some pretty long days. Anyway, I think an extra pair of hands might help. And I remembered how helpful Jackson was when I hung the Christmas lights."

She looked at her son's hopeful face. "Well, Jackson seems quite interested in helping you out and I'm fine with it." It was quickly settled—she would drop him in town tomorrow morning and Caleb would bring him home in the afternoon.

Jackson had just put away his phone when Oliver started barking frantically on the back porch. Taylor was pounding on the back door. "We need help," she told them with frightened eyes.

"What's wrong?" Jackson asked.

"My mom. She's really sick. I called Uncle Greg, but he hasn't called back. And I'm scared."

Wendy grabbed her coat and car keys. "Let's take the car in case she needs to go to the doctor."

They followed Taylor into the house to find Kara lying motionless on the sofa and Tessa standing beside her. "Kara?" Wendy asked. "Are you okay?"

Kara just groaned. "Sick," she mumbled. "Sick . . . my stomach."

"She's been throwing up," Taylor told Wendy. "A lot."

Wendy didn't know what to do, so she felt Kara's forehead, which was cool and clammy. "Should we take you to the doctor? Or the hospital?"

"No, no." Kara moaned. "Can't afford it."

"Do you know what made you sick?" Wendy hoped it wasn't alcohol or a hangover, but knew that was a possibility.

"Bad food," Kara said.

"What did you eat? Do you know?"

"Leftovers."

"I bet she brought something home from work last night." Taylor ran into the kitchen, then returned with a white takeout box. "Sometimes she brings food home." She held out the box like evidence then sniffed it. "Some kind of fish, I think."

"Is this what made you sick?" Wendy held the box so Kara could see.

"Ugh—yes—swordfish."

Wendy pulled out her phone and was soon talking to a poison control center. The woman was just telling her to get Kara in for medical help when Kara's brother burst into the house, demanding to know what was wrong. Taylor tearfully told him, and Wendy relayed what she'd just heard from the poison control woman.

"I'll take her to the ER," Greg told Wendy. "Can you take the girls to your house?"

"Yes, of course." Wendy nodded. "They can spend the night."

Greg scooped up Kara, whisking her away. Then Wendy helped Tessa and Taylor gather some overnight things.

Their little house was similar to hers, but it was sparse and barren—impoverished. She realized as they were locking up that it was also cold and damp—a rental cabin that had never been improved for year-round occupancy. What a sad way to live.

Wendy was glad she'd cleaned out the third bedroom for the Realtor's visit. She'd sorted, relocated, and given away all the stored items until she'd finally exposed a full-sized bed and several other pieces of bedroom furniture. As she led the girls to this "guest room," Wendy tried to reassure them that their mom would be okay. "Your uncle will make sure she gets good care." She watched as they set their things on the bed.

"We should all pray she gets well soon," Jackson told them.

"Good thinking," Wendy said. "Let's do that now." They all bowed their heads, praying that Kara would get good help, get well, and come home soon.

"Can we make Mommy some more sand dollar angels?" Tessa asked when they were done. "She really liked the ones we brought home."

"Yes," Wendy agreed. "And I'll cook us up a great big pan of homemade macaroni and cheese." She turned to Jackson. "How about if you get a fire going?"

All in all, it turned into a pleasant evening. Greg called to tell them that with an IV and some medication, Kara was going to be just fine and that she'd probably be released later that evening. "I'll keep the girls overnight just the same," Wendy told him.

By the time Wendy delivered the girls back to their house the next morning, along with their sand dollar angels, Kara looked weak but much improved. "I can't thank you enough."

She hugged Wendy. "I'm so lucky to have such good neighbors. Thank you so much!"

Still, as Wendy drove home after dropping Jackson off to work with Caleb, she felt like Kara's misfortune carried a serious warning. A single mom without good employment in a seasonal tourist town had some serious challenges to face. Kara had a brother to help her, but even so she'd been completely vulnerable yesterday. And Wendy had no family to fall back on. It was just her and Jackson. She knew it was her parental responsibility to make sure their life was as secure as possible. If the cottage sold today, that would be just fine!

She'd just gone inside the cottage when Sandi called to say that her buyers were in the Caribbean until next Wednesday. Wendy said that was fine, but as she put away her phone she felt severely disappointed. She was ready to wrap this up and return to Ohio ASAP. Well, except she still hadn't told Jackson. For that reason, she was grateful for the delay. She didn't relish the idea of the buyers poking around the cottage when Jackson came home. That would be awkward!

On Sunday morning, Jackson was up early, neatly dressed, and ready to go to church. "Taylor just texted me from her mom's phone," he said as they got into the car. "She wants to stay home with her mom today. But she promised to go to youth group with me next week."

"That's nice." Wendy pursed her lips, trying to think of an easy way to tell Jackson that they would probably be headed back to Ohio by next weekend. Later . . . she'd tell him after church.

"That storm's still not here," Jackson observed as she pulled into the parking lot.

"I just heard it's been circling the Atlantic and is supposed to hit midweek," she said as they got out.

"Cool. I can't wait to see what it does to the beach. We'll probably find all kinds of shells."

She just nodded, promising herself that she would tell Jackson the truth about selling the cabin this afternoon. They should have plenty of time to hash it out with no interruptions. But after church let out, while she and Jackson were visiting with Caleb, another distraction popped up.

"Mom's making clam chowder for lunch today," Jackson told Caleb. "It's her grandma's special recipe. You should come over and have some with us."

"Did you have success with your clam digging?" Caleb asked Jackson.

"No," Jackson admitted. "Mom's going to use canned clams."

"That sounds good to me." Caleb grinned hopefully at Wendy. "If you really want me to—"

"Yes, of course," she assured him. "Please, come join us for clam chowder. The clams might be canned, but the bacon is fresh." She smiled.

"How about I bring a good loaf of bread?"

She nodded. "Perfect."

As they drove home, she couldn't deny feeling relief at having one more excuse to delay what would be a hard conversation with Jackson. In fact, she wondered if the kindest thing would be to not say a word until the buyers actually made their cash offer—then just tell him, "It's a done deal and it's time to go." Sort of like ripping off a bandage. It might sting, but it wouldn't last long.

Caleb showed up with a big smile and a loaf of bread. "It

just hit me that you got to have my grandma's seafood stew and now I get to enjoy your grandma's clam chowder," he said as she led him inside. "Very nice."

To Wendy's delight, Caleb looked thoroughly impressed with the cottage as he removed his coat. "This place is *sweet*," he told both of them. "You guys do some seriously good work." He paused to admire the shell-framed mirror by the front door. "Wendy, did you make this?"

"She did," Jackson proudly informed him. "And all these other things too." Now he led Caleb around, showing him each handmade item and finally stopping in front of the Christmas tree.

Caleb let out a low whistle. "Man, that has got to be the prettiest Christmas tree I've ever seen."

"I cut it down myself," Jackson proclaimed.

"And these ornaments." Caleb pointed to a sand dollar angel. "Did you guys make these?"

"Mom made most of 'em. I helped a little, but it was her idea."

"Wendy." Caleb turned to face her. "You could easily sell those."

"Really?" She spilled out the story of taking them to his shop. "But you were gone and Crystal, uh, well, she didn't think they were so hot."

Caleb laughed. "Yeah, I'll bet she didn't. But if you want to sell them in my shop, I'd be proud to have them. And I plan to be open a lot between now and Christmas. Seems like the town has had more traffic than usual this year. I'm sure I could sell a lot of those during the next week. Hey, maybe I could get a tree to put in the window to display them on."

"I'll help you get a tree," Jackson offered. "I know where to go and everything."

"Great." Caleb turned to Wendy. "Bring in whatever you want on Tuesday and we'll get it all set up. And I'd love to consign some of your larger items too. I wouldn't be surprised if some got purchased as Christmas presents."

Wendy tried not to get her hopes up as they sat down together at the kitchen table. She'd done that too many times before . . . only to be disappointed. But as they bowed their heads to ask for God to bless the food, she silently prayed for a miracle. *Please, do something to allow us to stay here permanently,* she prayed with urgency. *Please, help us keep this happy home. Please!*

# Fourteen

ON TUESDAY MORNING, the predicted nor'easter was just starting to show its face. The sky was pewter gray and the wind was whipping the sea grass as Wendy drove to town. She'd loaded the back of her car with all her handcrafted treasures—some that she'd only just finished last night. But she was eager to get them unloaded before the storm cut loose.

Caleb met her outside, helping her carry the boxes and packages into the shop. And there in the center of the front window, just like Jackson had told her last night, stood a tall pine tree. "And lights too!" Wendy happily watched as Caleb plugged it in.

"Of course. Now if you don't mind, I'll leave you to it. Go ahead and decorate the tree and put your pieces wherever you think they best fit." Caleb showed her where he'd laid out the paperwork and price tags. "I'll be in my woodshop. And we don't officially open until ten, so no one should interrupt you."

She went right to work filling out the paperwork and putting on price tags, then carefully arranging and rearranging her various pieces. They really were perfect accents to Caleb's handmade furniture, and if just a couple pieces sold, well, she would have grocery money. Finally, she decorated the tree. Besides all the sand dollar angels, she'd made lots of shell decorations yesterday. As she stood back to admire it, she couldn't help but feel a flush of pride. It was even better than she'd expected.

"Wow!" Caleb came into the shop. "That is absolutely stunning, Wendy." He shook his head in disbelief as he came closer. "Seriously, it's beautiful. We need to be sure and get some photos." He looked around the shop to see where and how she'd placed her other pieces. "You have a real knack for this." He pointed to a shelf unit that she'd added items to. "Really nice touches! We better get some photos of those too."

She thanked him and was just handing him her paperwork when Crystal came in through the back door. "What have we here?" She unbuttoned her coat. "I noticed the Christmas tree from the street, and I must say it looks very festive. Nicely done, Caleb."

"This is Wendy's doing," he told her. Although Crystal acted like this was perfectly wonderful, Caleb exchanged glances with Wendy. "Come into my woodshop and we'll go over this paperwork." He led her to the back.

"I just want to thank you," Wendy said after he closed the door, "for giving me this chance, Caleb. You don't know how much it means to me."

"I'm happy to do it. Your things only make my shop look better." Suddenly his grin faded. "Hey, what's this?" He held up a page, pointing to the Ohio address she'd written on the line designated for mailing the check.

"I didn't want to have to tell you this," she began carefully, "mostly because Jackson doesn't even know about it yet, but I listed the cottage with a Realtor and I—"

"What? Are you serious?"

"I signed papers with Sandi Atkins last week, and she has a cash buyer that—"

"But what does that mean?" he demanded. "You and Jackson are leaving?"

"I'm supposed to report back to work before Christmas . . . in Cincinnati," she said. "According to Sandi, her buyers could be here in a couple days and she's pretty certain they'll want it and we can—"

"Of course they'll want it!" He was pacing now. "You've made the cottage so nice. Why wouldn't they want it? But I thought you did that for you and Jackson. I didn't realize you were *leaving* Seaside."

"I don't want to leave," she confessed. "That's what I was trying to tell you."

"But you're telling me that you're leaving." He ran his hands through his hair in frustration. "I just don't get it."

"I'm a single parent, Caleb. I have responsibilities to my son—"

"Yes. And your son loves it here in Seaside. Can't you see that?"

"Of course I can see that. But you don't understand. I still have huge medical bills from when my husband was sick. And there are college loans that still aren't paid off. I need a job that pays a family wage. Even then, without selling the cottage, I don't see how I'll ever get ahead." Now she told him about what happened with Kara over the weekend. "I keep thinking that could be me."

"But you said she was fine now."

"She is fine, but she lives on the edge. Tessa told me that if her mom's tips at the restaurant aren't good, they have to live on ramen noodles. I can't do that to Jackson."

"Maybe you should ask Jackson. Ramen noodles in Seaside might trump sirloin steak in Cincinnati!"

She was frustrated now, wishing she'd never said anything to him. The only reason she had was because he'd given her hope. She'd wanted to ask him if he thought she could really make it here—and if she should cancel her contract with Sandi. But he was so upset that all she wanted to do was get away.

"I'm sorry," he said. "I don't usually fly off the handle. But I feel sort of blindsided. I honestly didn't think you were leaving. Jackson sure doesn't."

"I know, and for the time being, we need to keep it that way." She sadly sighed. "Please, don't mention this to him."

"Right."

"Anyway, I just wanted to thank you for letting me put my things in your shop." Her eyes felt blurry as she stared down at the table he was currently working on. "And I know you're busy. I should let you get back to it. This is lovely by the way, and I know you've got a lot to get done before Christmas." She hurried out, and without saying a word to Crystal, grabbed up her coat and purse and ran outside.

As she drove home, she felt hot tears streaking down her cheeks. She hadn't expected Caleb to react like that. She'd thought he would understand. But then, he wasn't a dad. He was a "confirmed bachelor" who didn't have the kind of grown-up responsibilities she had. But witnessing his strong reaction reminded her that Jackson's would be even worse. Oh, why did this have to be so hard?

Wendy had no incentive to do anything back at the cottage. Instead, she simply walked around and around, with Oliver trailing her. As she walked, she stared at all the projects she and Jackson had worked so hard to complete—knowing full well that the cash buyers would probably just tear it all out anyway. Based on Sandi's comments about deep pockets and expensive taste, this cottage would probably be completely gutted in a week or two. If they paid her cash on Thursday, they could be tearing into it as soon as this weekend. It made her want to scream.

The bare and unlit Christmas tree felt like a metaphor for her life. She wished she hadn't taken all of her ornaments to Caleb's shop. What difference would it make whether they sold or not? And with the nor'easter just starting to bear down, it was unlikely that holiday shoppers would be around. The sooner she and Jackson got out of here, the better it would be—for everyone. And yet the idea of saying goodbye to Caleb—if he would even talk to her again—made her feel sick inside.

As she continued to pace back and forth through the house, watching with only mild interest as the rain came down in sheets, she remembered that Jackson was supposed to work with Caleb after school, and that Caleb planned to deliver him home after five. Would this be her last chance to repair the rift between her and Caleb? Was it worth trying to make him understand? What if she ran out to meet him? She could apologize profusely—and invite him for dinner. And who knew where it might go from there?

Fueled with hope and fresh urgency, Wendy went into action making more tree ornaments. No reason she and Jackson shouldn't enjoy their Christmas tree while they could. At a little before four, she cleaned up her crafting things, tidied the house, and started organizing for dinner, even putting cloth napkins and candles on the kitchen table. As she stirred the meat sauce, she hoped Caleb liked spaghetti as much as Jackson did. It was nearly five when she got a fire going in the fireplace. Then with everything sweetly ready and in place, she waited by the front window, her coat ready to throw on when Caleb showed up with Jackson. Perhaps the pouring rain would gain her some sympathy when she apologized. She would insist Caleb join them for dinner, and with Jackson watching, how could he refuse?

But five o'clock came and went. She fed Oliver and put another log on the fire and then, at five thirty, she texted Jackson, telling him that dinner was ready and it was okay to invite Caleb. When she didn't hear back from him, she grew concerned. She called Jackson's number, and when it went straight to voice mail, she grew even more worried. She called Caleb's number and, relieved to hear his voice, inquired about Jackson.

"Jackson?" He sounded slightly disoriented.

"My son," she clarified with a bit of irritation. "Your able-bodied assistant. Remember?"

"Jackson hasn't been here. He didn't show up for work."

"What do you mean?" she demanded.

"I mean he's not here, Wendy. I haven't seen him today."

Her heart began to pound as she stared out to where the storm was raging with a vengeance. "Then where . . . where is he?" she asked in a tiny voice. "I, uh, I gotta go." She hung up and tried to think. Where was Jackson? Of course, *Taylor*—he had to be with Taylor. She called Kara's number, trying to keep her voice calm as she asked.

"I'm sorry, Wendy. I haven't seen Jackson today."

So Wendy asked to speak to Taylor, pressing her about Jackson's whereabouts. "He didn't ride the bus home," Taylor explained. "He stayed in town. He was going to Caleb's shop to help him today."

"Oh." Wendy felt tightness in her chest. "Okay then, if you happen to hear from him, please tell him to call me." Still clutching her phone, she ran outside to where the wind was howling and sleet was mixing with the rain. Standing on the porch, she helplessly looked all around. Oliver, shivering beside her, seemed to be anxiously looking too. "Where is he, boy?" she asked in desperation. "Where is Jackson?"

Her phone jangled, making her jump. "Jackson?" she said without even checking the caller ID.

"It's Caleb. What's going on, Wendy?"

"He's not here! He never came home on the bus. Taylor said he stayed in town—to work with you. And there's— this—this storm!" She burst into tears. "Oh, *where* is he?"

"I'm on my way! I'll search along the road as I drive. And I'll call my friend Jim Burns. He's the Seaside sheriff, and he can let his guys know to be on the lookout. We'll find him."

She thanked him, then shaking from fear and trembling from cold, she went back into the house. Where could Jackson be? Had he been kidnapped? In a small town like Seaside? It made no sense. But why would he stay in town and not go to Caleb's shop? He loved working with Caleb. And to take off on foot in this storm? Nothing made sense. *Please, God.* She got down on her knees next to the sofa. *Please, get him home safely to me. Please, please, please!*

She was still praying when Caleb arrived. "Did you find him?" she demanded as she opened the door, letting the wind and Caleb in, peering over his shoulder, hoping to spot her son loping up the walk.

"No. I didn't see anyone walking out there—not in this weather."

"What about your sheriff friend?" She closed the door against the wind. "Does he know anything? Do you think Jackson could've been kidnapped?"

"Jim's on it, Wendy. He's told all his men to be looking. And he said there've been no reports of anything out of the ordinary or suspicious lately. Seaside is a small town," he assured her. "Nothing goes unobserved here—and there has never been a kidnapping."

"Then where is my son?" She dissolved into tears again.

"Would he have any reason to, uh, run away?" Caleb's tone was cautious.

"Run away?" She blinked, wiping her tears with her hands. "Are you serious?"

"Jim asked me to ask you. He said that when kids his age go missing, nine times out of ten, it's a runaway."

"Jackson would *not* run away."

"No, I didn't think so." Caleb unzipped his jacket. "He seems like a well-adjusted young man."

Wendy stared out the window. "Maybe I should go out there and look for him."

"Where would you look?"

"On the beach?"

"In the dark? In this storm? Plus, it's high tide right now. Pretty soon we'd be looking for you. And by then Jackson would probably be sitting by that fire all warm and dry. No, you just need to stay put and let the sheriff's department handle this."

"Where will they look?"

"Jim said they'll check out the typical places, around the school, and the arcade and burger joint—wherever kids hang out."

"Taylor said he stayed in town to work with you this afternoon," Wendy told him again. "Are you absolutely certain he didn't show up? Maybe you'd stepped out or—"

"I was in my woodshop all day. Jackson never came."

"Maybe Crystal saw him," she tried. "Was she there this afternoon? Did you ask her if she'd seen him?"

"She'd already gone home by the time you called me." He pulled out his phone. "But I'll call and ask her." Wendy listened anxiously as Caleb explained the situation and how worried they were. "He came into the store?" Caleb locked eyes with Wendy as he listened. "Why didn't you send him back to my woodshop?" His mouth grew firm as he waited. "What did you say to him, Crystal? *Tell me right now!*" He listened a bit longer, then without saying goodbye, he hung up.

"What is it?" Wendy demanded.

"A pretty important piece of the puzzle." He pursed his lips, rubbing his chin.

"What is it, Caleb? Tell me!"

"Crystal was making small talk with Jackson, and she let it slip that you were selling the cottage and you guys were moving back to Ohio."

Wendy felt a surge of rage well up in her. "How on earth did Crystal know about that? Did you tell her?"

"No. She admitted that she overheard us in the woodshop this morning. In other words, she was *eavesdropping*." He pounded a fist into his palm. "And interfering. Believe me,

Crystal will be unemployed tomorrow." He put his hand on her shoulder. "The good news is that he hasn't been kidnapped, Wendy."

"That's true." She nodded, still feeling shaky. "Did Crystal say how Jackson reacted to this news?"

"She said he didn't believe her at first. And then, he was pretty upset. I think she actually felt a little guilty."

"I'm the one who should feel guilty." Wendy made her way to the sofa, sinking into it with trembling knees. "This is all my fault. I should've made it perfectly clear instead of allowing him to hope there was a chance we could stay. I'm such a coward. Such a lousy mom."

He sat next to her, slipping an arm around her shoulders. "You're a good mom, Wendy."

"I'm a dishonest mom." She turned to look at him. "But I thought it was for his own good. I really did." And like a cork popped off a bottle, she spilled out the whole story— how Jackson had been so down after Edward died, how he'd changed and been hurt by his peers and started to hate school. "But when he thought we were moving here, he completely perked up. It was like a miracle. He was so happy . . . I just hated to burst his balloon." She wiped her tears on her sleeve. "And now this." She stared down at her phone. "Jackson, where are you?" She texted him again. This time she told him she was sorry she hadn't been more definite about selling the cottage, begging him to call so they could talk and telling him that she loved him.

"Okay," Caleb said calmly. "Let's assume this *is* a runaway situation. Jackson was obviously upset . . . perhaps he was very angry at you . . . he didn't want to go home . . . So where would he go?"

"Taylor was my first guess, but she hadn't seen him since earlier."

Caleb continued to question her, trying to dig out any clues there were—but there just weren't any. Then he called his sheriff friend, explaining that it might be a runaway situation after all. He was just hanging up when Wendy's phone jangled. It was Kara on the other end. "Taylor just confessed to me that she's been hiding Jackson in our shed, Wendy."

"Is he okay?"

"Hungry and cold, but he's fine. And Taylor said to tell you she's very sorry. Jackson swore her to secrecy. But she said you've been such a good friend to us that she felt too guilty."

"I'm on my way!" Wendy thanked her and hung up.

"I'll drive you," Caleb offered. "Unless you'd rather I didn't. I don't want to force my way into your family business."

"I wish you'd stick around." She pulled on her coat then smiled. "You're the closest thing we have to family right now."

He smiled back. "That's nice to hear."

After a silent drive home, the three of them sat in the living room with the Christmas tree twinkling cheerfully on one side, the fireplace crackling on the other, and Oliver sleeping peacefully by the hearth. But with somber faces and downward glances, no one looked likely to speak.

Finally, Wendy decided to initiate the conversation by confessing and apologizing to Jackson. She poured out her story, explaining how being disingenuous had been tearing her apart. "I kept meaning to make you understand we could never stay here," she finally said. "But I knew it would only make you miserable." She wiped a tear. "And it was so nice seeing you happy. I love you so much. I just wanted you to be happy, Jackson. And if I could pull a miracle out of thin air, it would be for us to stay here forever, but I'm sorry, I just can't do—"

"I have a confession to make too, Mom," Jackson interrupted. "I knew all along you planned to sell the cottage."

"You really knew?"

"Yeah. You pretty much told me from the start," he reminded her. "And you tried to remind me lots of times, but I kept twisting it into what *I* wanted to happen. I thought I could convince you, make you want to stay. And it seemed like I was making good progress." He jerked his thumb toward Caleb. "I even tried to get you interested in him, hoping that would make you want to stay."

"Really?" Caleb's brows rose.

"Remember the night I wanted to stay home with Oliver?" Jackson's smile grew mischievous. "I just wanted you two to have a real date."

"I suspected as much," Wendy admitted.

"We did have a nice evening," Caleb reminded her. "And since everyone is making confessions, maybe I should make mine too."

"What?" they both said in unison.

"When I asked for Jackson to help me with the lights on my store that day, well, I didn't *really* need help. I just wanted an excuse to see Jackson's mom again."

"Oh, I knew that." Jackson waved a hand.

"But then I saw what a hard worker you were," Caleb continued. "And I really did want your help in my woodshop. In fact, I missed you today."

"I'm sorry." Jackson turned back to Wendy with sad eyes. "So, it's really true, Mom? You sold this place to some rich people?"

"Well, it's not sold yet. But we do have a potential buyer."

"And we're going back—back to Ohio?" His eyes were filling with tears now.

"We don't really have a choice, Jackson."

"What about Oliver?" Jackson pointed to the oblivious dog sleeping by the fire. "Does that mean I have to give him up? I don't get my dog *and* I have to go back to Ohio? This is going to be the worst Christmas ever!"

Wendy didn't know what to say. "I'm sorry, son. I was imagining ways we could try to make this work—and I was taking your advice about trusting God to take care of us. I made those items to sell in town." She felt a painful lump in her throat. "But the fact is—I've got to make the responsible decision here. It's not easy being an adult. Someday, you'll understand that better." She swallowed hard as she reached for her son's hand. "I really don't have any other options. I'm expected at work. We have to go back."

"Not if I have anything to say about it," Caleb declared.

They both turned to stare at him.

Wendy noticed that his cheeks were flushed, probably from the fire. But it was his eyes that drew her attention. They were clear and bright—and intense.

"What do you mean?" Jackson demanded.

"Well, I've been thinking about your, uh, situation too," Caleb said slowly, looking from Jackson to Wendy. "I've actually given it a fair amount of thought these past two weeks." He pointed to the Christmas tree. "For starters, Wendy, I never got the chance to tell you that in just one day I must've sold a couple dozen of your Christmas tree ornaments."

"Really?" She felt a tinge of hope.

He nodded. "Maybe more. And remember the couple that

you helped in my store the other day, the ones who ordered the dining table?"

"Yes." She waited.

"Well, they loved your mirror and the husband told me on the sly that he plans to come get it for his wife for a Christmas present."

"Seriously?" She felt a bigger rush of hope.

"So, I honestly think there's a future for you here in Seaside," he declared.

"I'd like to believe that."

"Listen to him!" Jackson leaped to his feet, going over to the tree where she'd added more decorations earlier. "These are so cool, Mom. I'll bet you sell every single one by Christmas."

"That would certainly help," she admitted. "But it's not the same as a full-time job with benefits."

"I'll be looking for someone to replace Crystal in my shop," Caleb told her. "It's not full-time, and I don't have much in the way of benefits. Although you'd get commission."

She considered this. As badly as she wanted to remain in Seaside, to carve out a new life, she still had Jackson's future to consider.

"And you have a marketing background," Caleb continued. "Maybe you could help me in that department too. I could sure use it."

She brightened. "I was wondering why you don't have a website or even a catalogue."

"Because I never have time to set that stuff up." He held up his hands. "Or the know-how."

"Come on, Mom," Jackson urged. "Please say we can stay here."

"As much as I'd love to say yes, I'm the grown-up in this family, Jackson. I have to do what's best for—"

"Okay." Caleb stood, holding up both hands with an uncertain expression. "I doubt this is the proper way to do this. And I'd really been planning on something more romantic— like on Christmas Eve." Caleb dropped down on one knee. But instead of facing Wendy, he turned to Jackson. "I'd like to ask your permission to marry your mother, Jackson."

Jackson's whole face lit up. "Really? You mean it?"

"I absolutely mean it."

"Yeah!" Jackson nodded. "Well, if it's all right with Mom. I guess you should ask her too."

Caleb pivoted around to face her. "Wendy, I know this must seem sudden to you, but something inside me clicked that day we met in the hardware store. Remember, when you thought I was a pesky salesman?"

"But you won me over," she said quietly, trying to absorb what was happening.

"I won you over?" he repeated with hopeful eyes. "So will you? Wendy, will you *please* marry me?"

Wendy was speechless. "Wait a minute." Her voice trembled with emotion. "Is this a *pity proposal*? Because if it is, I can't possibly—"

"I assure you, this is *not* a pity proposal." He reached for her hand with both of his. "I love you, Wendy. I love you from the bottom of my heart. I think I fell for you almost as soon as we met. I want you for my wife. And I want Jackson for my son." He paused. "But I realize this is sudden. If you need some time to think about it, I'll understand and—"

"Yes!" Falling to her knees next to him, Wendy threw her arms around him, and right there in front of her son, they kissed. "Yes, Caleb, I do love you!" she declared. "And I do want to marry you."

Jackson let out a loud cheer, rousing Oliver from his snooze. Suddenly the three of them, with Oliver bouncing about their heels, were all dancing around the room in joyful celebration.

"God really did it, Mom!" Jackson shouted. "He answered my prayers!"

"Mine too," Caleb said with his arm still around Wendy.

"Mine too," Wendy confirmed.

"Yours too." Jackson hugged Oliver. "We're all going to have the best Christmas ever!"

**Melody Carlson** is the award-winning author of over two hundred books, including *Christmas at Harrington's*, *The Christmas Pony*, *A Simple Christmas Wish*, *The Christmas Cat*, *The Christmas Joy Ride*, *The Christmas Angel Project*, and *The Christmas Blessing*. Melody has received a Romantic Times Career Achievement Award in the inspirational market for her books. She and her husband live in central Oregon. For more information about Melody, visit her website at www.melodycarlson.com.

She's determined to give her baby a better life.

# COULD A CHRISTMAS MIRACLE MAKE IT POSSIBLE?

# Perfect for readers who want a *heartwarming and hopeful Christmas story.*

Inspired by their late friend's gifts for them, four members of a book club decide to become someone's Christmas angel—and find their own lives are changed.

# More Christmas Adventures from
## Melody Carlson!

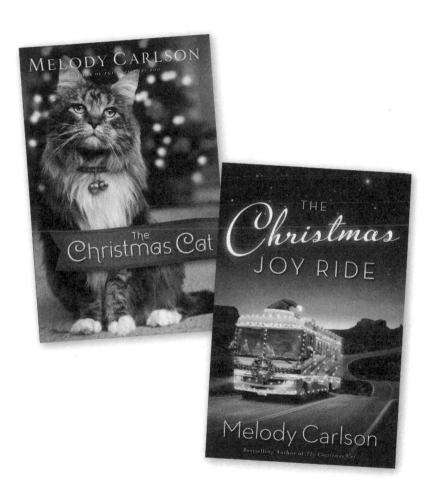

# New Places. New Adventures. New Love.

MELODY CARLSON

*A New York City Romance*

*Once Upon a Summertime*

MELODY CARLSON

*A San Francisco Romance*

*All Summer Long*

MELODY CARLSON

*A Savannah Romance*

*Under a Summer Sky*

MEET
# Melody

MelodyCarlson.com